Old Buildings in North Texas

JEN WALDO has lived in Holland, Egypt, the UK, Scotland, Kuwait and Singapore, but now lives in her home state of Texas, where her novels are set.

She first began writing twenty-five years ago, and shortly afterwards one of her stories was picked up by *The European* and was shortlisted in a competition by *Traveler*.

Her forthcoming second novel, *Why Stuff Matters*, is also published by Arcadia Books.

Old Buildings in North Texas

JEN WALDO

A

Arcadia Books Ltd
139 Highlever Road
London W10 6PH

www.arcadiabooks.co.uk

First published in Great Britain 2016
This B format edition published 2017

Copyright © Jen Waldo 2016

ISBN 978-1-911350-17-0

Typeset in Garamond by MacGuru Ltd
Printed and bound by TJ International, Padstow PL28 8RW

ARCADIA BOOKS DISTRIBUTORS ARE AS FOLLOWS:

in the UK and elsewhere in Europe:
BookSource
50 Cambuslang Road
Cambuslang
Glasgow G32 8NB

in Australia/New Zealand:
NewSouth Books
University of New South Wales
Sydney NSW 2052

Old Buildings in North Texas

To my husband, David, who encourages and supports me every day, who believes in me when I don't believe in myself, and who helps me find my way from one end of a plot to the other.

The Situation

Before they'd let me out of rehab someone had to agree to act as my legal custodian. There it is, the snappy truth about why, at the age of thirty-two, I live with my mother. She now has control over every aspect of my life, from my finances to my laundry. One little cocaine-induced heart attack and it's back to my childhood to start over.

Jane, my therapist, says I need to acquire a hobby. Apparently deep introspection while smoking cigarettes and drinking coffee doesn't count. So far I've dabbled in eschatology, zombie lore, and, just lately because it's an election year, politics.

"Maybe you should look into something a little less doomsday, something that doesn't make everybody around you wish you'd go somewhere else," Jane says. She disapproves of my libertarian leanings.

"Give me a list, Jane," I tell her. "Give me a list of hobbies that'll be acceptable to absolutely every person who has a say in every choice I make every single minute of every day."

Beth Ann, the neighbor across the street from the house I grew up in and have returned to, makes quilts, vivid intricate quilts with evocative names like log cabin, nine patch, and saw-tooth stars. She ran out of people to give them to years ago and now when she finishes one she stores it in a

< 1 >

mid-sized room that holds nothing but quilts, from floor to ceiling, from one side to the other, from back to front.

Her husband, Jerry, builds birdhouses – delicate abodes all decked out like human homes with tiny porches, painted shutters, and tile roofs. They, too, take up a lot of space – two whole walls of shelves in the garage, which Jerry turned into his work area in the early nineties. As to their purpose, I'm dubious. Quilts I can see a use for; decorated bird-houses, not so much.

Another result of addiction is court-mandated counsel-ing. It's hard for me to take my assigned therapist, Jane Gilley, seriously. We whispered and giggled together during two years of Mr. Finch's AP English. Now she looks at me with eyes so empathetic and wise that I want to throw some-thing at her. She's gained weight and her hair is lighter than it used to be. On her desk sits a family portrait – Jane and her husband posing behind their two fair-haired children, each parent with a hand on the shoulder of a child. She keeps the picture turned toward us as we have our session, glancing at it every once in a while, seeking relief from my overflowing bitterness.

"Are you writing in your journal?"

"Every day." This is a lie. Why would I want a record of this hell?

"Good. I'd think, as a writer, you'd find it cathartic." She shifts, glances toward her lap, offering body language I can't interpret. "We need to examine the background of your addiction."

Convinced that there's some complex and profound neurosis behind my dependency, she brings this up every session. At her suggestion, I've contemplated my life before my fall into the abyss. Was I feeling empty? Was I seeking solace for some heartbreak or failure? Was I depressed and

< 2 >

self-medicating? No. I was happy, climbing in my profession. My call on this is a simple one – I forgot who I was. I lost control. I wasn't vigilant. When I've shared this insight with Jane, she's been unsupportive and disbelieving. She wants me to dig deeper, to present her with some long-buried pain or lack of fulfillment. Stubborn, she persists in her conviction that I am a bottomless well rather than a shallow pond.

"I hate the pills." The two medications I'm on are standard – Xanax regulates my mind while Propranolol regulates my heart. Both make me feel exhausted and both give me insomnia. The result is a feeling of constant detachment, like I'm not even present in my own life.

"You really need to stick with the regime," she says. "But for today, time's up."

And I'm out of there. All the money I had in my bank account three months ago is gone. What didn't go up my nose went to medical and legal costs, and I'm still deeply in debt. But I was lucky enough to implode before losing my car, a Honda Accord that I bought new three years ago. Now, because it's all that belongs to me in the whole world, I'm excessively appreciative. I wash and vacuum it weekly, check it daily for scratches, talk to it as though it's my only friend.

I wonder if car care counts as a hobby. I'll ask Jane at our next session.

In Dallas I worked as the regulars' editor for *Dallas Flair*, a local fashion magazine. It was my dream career, a grand life in the making. Here in Caprock, with my background (and I am impressive – BA in English from Rice, MA in Journalism from Columbia, *magna cum laude* in both) I should've been able to get a job on the newspaper, the *Caprock Chronicle*, which, as far as I can tell, is none too

< 3 >

choosy. And there's a local magazine here, too, that I'm well-suited for. Called *Caprock Comfort*, it has more to do with home decorating than fashion, but still, it's work I could do, a theme I could get behind. I like comfort as much as the next person.

Oddly, the reason I'm not working for one of these publications isn't because I'm an addict or that I'm unqualified. It's because I left the area.

"Tech not good enough for you?" asked Stanley Mason, editor of the *Caprock Chronicle*. "Most of our staff went to Tech. Or Pan UT." Located two hours to the south, Texas Tech is as far as most people from Caprock go for their higher education. And Pan UT, the panhandle branch of the University of Texas system, is even closer – half an hour to the southwest, in Gorman.

"Columbia? Isn't that in New York?" asked Susan Riley, editor of *Caprock Comfort*. "Why'd you go way up there? That must have been horrible."

One of the requirements of addiction recovery is gainful employment so, because I couldn't get a job in my field, my mom imposed on her oldest and best friend, Zachary Palin, who has been a surrogate father to my sister Chloe and me. A famous jewelry designer, Zachary has a store in the mall and he's quite happy for me to stand behind the counter and wait on people when they wander in.

"Please, please, protect me from the public," was his entreaty when I went to talk to him about the job.

I love Zachary. He's eccentric, self-absorbed, and composed primarily of affectations – a scrawny white ponytail that hangs from the back of his tall Stetson; a classic red bandana knotted at his saggy throat; a plaid shirt with pearl snaps; a wide belt with a massive buckle he designed himself; faded Levi 501s; and brown hand-crafted boots

< 4 >

with worn heels. And beneath the cowboy artifices, his heart is huge and loyal and generous. Giving me this job is only one of the million things he's done for me since I was a child.

I rush into the store, racing the second hand to the twelve. There are no customers. It looks like Zachary hasn't completed opening shop – the recessed lighting hasn't been turned on and the air is still stale. Perched on the elevated stool behind the central register, Zachary is talking on the phone.

"I won't make them without meeting the two of you as a couple," he says. Watching my arrival, he rolls his eyes, communicating how difficult it is to be so wonderful, so in demand. "Of course I'll come to you, just like last time. Let me know well in advance because my schedule is very full."

It's not unusual for Zachary to take off for distant shores to discuss wedding rings with celebs. It's a lucrative business. Zachary owns three Cadillacs and the largest house in Goodnight Hills, the affluent residential estate west of town. In contrast, this store in the mall makes no money whatsoever. When I asked him why he keeps it, he said it's because he needs a place to go when he isn't at home or at our house. His daily routine is a triangle.

I stuff my purse into the box safe in the back room, clock in, and return to the front. Zachary's off the phone.

"Who's the latest client and where?" I ask, flicking the switch for the showcase lights and scanning the area to see what my first chores will be. There are fingerprints on the glass case over by the door. I grab the cleaner and cloth from beneath the counter and aim myself toward the offending smudges.

"Costa Rica. Grace Alonza and Burnett Tow." A movie star and an NFL player.

< 5 >

"I thought they were both married to other people."

"Not for long. I did the rings for both their marriages, so they're repeat customers, which says something, I suppose. But I'm disappointed the first rings didn't take. I'm going to design the next ones with fidelity as the first priority."

That's Zachary's gimmick – he claims to contemplate the combined aura of the couple and infuse the metals of the rings with the spiritual qualities most conducive to a successful relationship for the individuals involved. What a lot of hooey. Only superstars can afford to be so gullible.

"Jane says I need a hobby," I tell him.

"Everybody needs something to pass the time until they die," he says.

"Do you have a hobby?"

"I design wedding rings for rich people."

And with this irritating assertion hanging in the air, he meanders out into the mall, scuffing the heels of his cowboy boots toward the food court where he'll flirt with the new hire at the cookie place, a pretty seventeen-year-old boy with golden hair, clear skin, and tight glutes.

< 6 >

Why Me?

I miss cocaine. I miss the way it made me feel intimately connected to the most distant corners of the universe. I miss the way it made me more than what I was. I worked better, moved quicker, looked classier, sounded smarter. Everything I did was thrilling and brilliant.

And if occasionally I felt jittery and angry, or if every once in a while I caught the shadow of a monster dancing at the edge of my periphery, it was worth it. I told myself that I wasn't addicted – right up until I was seized by a pain in my chest so powerful and terrifying that I thought I was dying. And I was.

Now instead of using, I long to use. Instead of flying, I'm grounded by the dull drag of the earth's core. I was told the need would grow less intense with time. And it has. At first I felt like I was missing half my soul. Now I only feel like a quarter of me's gone. A few months ago the craving was constant. Now I can go five minutes at a time without hearing the seductive sigh of my most cherished friend.

And these days my paycheck goes straight into my mother's hands rather than into the hands of various friends; and by friends I mean dealers. In an effort to avoid the humiliation of bankruptcy, and also because she believes that honorable people meet their financial obligations, Mom sits down with me weekly and goes over my finances,

< 7 >

meticulously allocating and writing out checks to all the people I owe. Most of the debt is medical – eight hundred for the ambulance, twelve thousand to the hospital, thirteen thousand to the rehab facility. Also there's about ten thousand in unpaid credit card debt and a couple of thousand I borrowed from friends. Debt is an insurmountable wall between me and my future.

Mom also organizes my doses of medication into small click-top containers, doling them out daily, not even able to trust me with my own stupid pills. Her fingers are thinner than they once were and the blue veins on the back of her hands are more prominent, but she is still youthful and strong, still in complete charge of her world.

I wasn't the only one who used. I didn't know a single person who didn't amp on a regular basis. Co-workers, friends I went out with, people I saw occasionally, people I saw every day – they all used. Now I'm forbidden to communicate with any of them. Am I resentful? Hell yes. Why did this happen to me and not Mary, who won't even get out of bed until she has, as she puts it, found her center; or Erik, whose feet haven't touched the ground in five years? Why does one person fall hard when another doesn't stumble at all? This is one of the issues I'm supposed to be dealing with in therapy, but so far Jane seems to be mainly focused on replacing my bad habit with a healthy one.

"I think Jane's on the right track with her hobby idea," my mother says. "But my theory is that when you're depressed you should do something for someone else. Helping people lends perspective. Why don't you volunteer at the shelter on Fillmore?"

"A high percentage of people at shelters are addicts. Jane would not approve. And I'm not depressed."

< 8 >

"Sure you are. Look at all you've lost. Just thinking about your life depresses me and I'm not even the one living it." She's confused and disappointed. What happened to her golden daughter? Her misplaced expectations make me ache all over.

We're sitting on the patio in back of the house. Evenings in Caprock can be pleasant this time of year. Around seven o'clock, after a day of oppressive heat, a playful breeze begins to push the air around and the temperature drops several degrees. During the full light of day everything looks brown and dry, but when the pink sun sinks to the edge of the sky the teasing shadows can fool a person into seeing the leaves of the trees and the blades of grass as vivid green; it's an illusion, but an enjoyable one.

Mom's having a glass of wine and I'm having herbal tea. No wine for me – doesn't mix with my meds. With my laptop open on the table, I'm clicking through internet sites looking at hobby possibilities.

"Skydiving," Mom suggests. "That'd give you the rush you seem to crave."

"Looked into it. Can't afford it." She doesn't seem to comprehend that it doesn't matter what I do, there will be no rush for me. My mood and heart rate are so pharmaceutically regulated these days that nothing gets me excited.

"How about starting a collection?"

"Of what? Spoons? Stamps? Shouldn't a collection be something you care about?"

"Well then, what do you care about?"

"Candycaine, gutter glitter, wacky dust, rail." When did I become so snide? I clarify – "Cocaine, Mom. I care about cocaine."

"You've been down that road and look where it got you."

I'm being bitchy and she's losing patience. I light a

< 9 >

cigarette, inhale deeply, release a cloud. There are issues between us that we don't address. She feels helpless, which she hates; so there's resentment. She wonders where she was when I was getting in too deep. She thinks she failed as a mother, that if I was unprepared it's because she didn't prepare me; so there's guilt. Also, my weakness has made her overly protective. She's a hawk and I'm her chick.

"I hate that you smoke."

"One vice at a time," I tell her for the hundredth time. I, too, hate that I smoke. The only place to smoke at work is outside in the cruel sun, in an allocated square of sidewalk fifty feet from the north entrance. People glare and circle at a distance, offended by the smoke. I'm ostracized.

Also, Mom's a nurse in the pulmonary unit of the hospital, which means she's more aware than most of the damage cigarettes cause.

"Look at this one," I say. "If that's not a worthwhile hobby I don't know what is."

I turn the computer toward her. Two overweight bearded men gaze proudly from the screen. They're standing behind a replica of the bat cave they made out of Lego, a project that, according to the accompanying article, took an eight-hundred-hour chunk out of their lives.

"Hello? Ya'll back here?" Zachary's voice reaches us only seconds before the gate creaks open and his head pops through.

"Olivia needs a hobby," Mom tells him.

"So I heard." He comes fully through the gate and pulls it closed behind him. He's changed his cowboy shirt for a vintage Grateful Dead T-shirt, but the jeans, boots, bandana, and Stetson remain. Approaching, he holds out a bottle of cabernet.

"So far we've got Lego and collecting street names for

< 10 >

cocaine." Mom accepts the wine, rises, and crosses to the door to go inside and uncork it.

Zachary collapses into the third seat, leans back, and crosses his ankle over his knee. He comes over most evenings.

"Karen closing tonight?" Karen is his other clerk. With a worn face and achy movements, she looks and acts older than she is. I was surprised the other day to learn that she's thirty-six. I'd thought she was around fifty.

"Yep."

I turn the computer screen toward him so he can see the middle-aged geeks with their Lego.

"Wow," he says. "Which bat cave? There are so many. This is so cool." He pulls the computer toward him, hunches and squints, then proceeds to read the entire accompanying article. What a nerd.

After a few minutes Mom comes back out, places a glass of red on the table in front of Zachary, and once again takes her seat.

I regain my laptop and continue to click through hobby blogs as Mom and Zachary share news about their day. As usual, their words bump in mid-air without any real exchange of ideas. Zachary complains because the mayor's daughter has asked him to make the rings for her upcoming nuptials, but she feels she should get a discount because she's local and local people can't afford to pay what movie stars pay. And Mom says how someone in the neighborhood turns their dog loose every morning and what does the dog do? Heads straight to our yard to do its business. She's mentioned this several times and I honestly don't know what she can do to stop it.

I'm amazed by how many meaningless things people do to pass the time. Shouldn't life be more about living than

< 11 >

filling the hours? There are thousands and thousands of hobbies – passive ones like building collections, making scrapbooks, and cutting coupons; and more adventurous ones like mountain climbing, skateboarding, and cave diving. None of this appeals; I am lazy with an exaggerated fear of pain. I carry my search into even more extreme categories – wild animal taming, storm chasing, bungee jumping, and – hang on. Here's an intriguing one that takes very little, if any, outlay of cash.

Urban exploration. Urbexing. Finding ways into abandoned buildings and sneaking around. In essence, trespassing. It sounds bizarre and dirty. Rats and spiders would be involved. I'm fascinated. The construction of a building is a grand undertaking. Creating a structure consumes manpower and money. There're so many factors involved – land and materials, plumbing and electricity, planning, red tape, and occupancy. A building has value. And then it's just left as it stands, relinquished to the elements. Why?

I guess I inadvertently signal interest by shifting or blinking, because when I look up Mom and Zachary are staring at me.

"What?" I ask.

"Did something catch your attention?" Big-eyed and leaning toward me, Mom looks so hopeful.

"No." Feeling guilty for no reason, I quickly close the screen. She would be appalled to think I was even considering such a thing.

Lately I've been so self-absorbed that I've forgotten one of the qualities I enjoy most about myself – my curiosity. When I'm not awash in self-pity, or when I'm not obsessing over my lost friend, Big Bloke, I cultivate a lively interest in things that are absolutely none of my business. Some would say I'm nosy. I love thinking about how other

< 12 >

people live. I want to know what thoughts go through their heads as they work on Lego projects and make quilts and birdhouses. I want to understand motives and reactions, emotions and priorities. The concept of exploring a building where people used to create or labor, or a home where people slept, ate, and watched television offers me a whole new playground, an enticing distraction for someone who desperately needs one. And a specific house east of town has been whispering my name since I was a little girl.

< 13 >

The Meskar Place

Ten miles east of town, situated a half-mile off FM 92 and surrounded by six thousand acres of grazing land, is the Meskar Mansion. Mansion is a misnomer, due more to a local fondness for alliteration than design or proportion; in fact, if compared in size to the new homes going up on the west side, it's quite modest. Built in the nineteen-twenties, it's reminiscent of an era and culture alien to the Texas panhandle. With soaring columns, dormer windows, and a wrap-around balcony trimmed with intricately molded iron, the elegant structure evokes visions of genteel southern belles, arrogant pasty-faced men, and dark slaves who were either content or rabid, depending on their natures. But while the rich soil of the south nourishes magnolia trees, clinging honeysuckle, and Spanish moss, the hard hostile dirt of northern Texas supports only mesquite, a gnarled shrub that offers no beauty or grace. And so the grand plantation home stands alone with no chlorophyll to frame it, no festooned branches to enhance its lines.

There is no great mystery surrounding the house that would account for my interest, except that it's unique in the area and was once inhabited by people who were rich and powerful, and that thirty years ago the owner, Eubert Meskar, sole and final heir to the Meskar fortune, locked the doors and left in a huff.

< 14 >

I park on a side road, half a mile east of the house. A tumbleweed pirouettes across the hood of my Honda. Barbed wire stretches in front and behind as far as I can see. My car will be visible – everything's visible on this flat, flat land – but it's off the main road so it won't draw attention.

Dressed in jeans and a T-shirt, with my hiking boots to see me through any catastrophe my feet may encounter, I'm desperate for an adventure. A backpack is flopped sideways on the passenger seat. In it are a few items the advisory website said I would need – a flashlight, Band-Aids, a phone, and leather work gloves.

I've chosen to ignore two recommendations – the first being that I tell someone where I'm going, the second that I take a partner. Who would I tell? Who would I take? The people who used to know me don't want to know me now.

Backpack in hand, I emerge and circle the car. As intended, the fence is a deterrent – but not an overwhelming one. Tossing the backpack over the fence, I get a foothold on the rear bumper, clamber to the trunk, then to the roof. Scooting to the right, I position my heels on the lower window frame, and push off, landing with an "*oof!*" on the other side. See? Easily done, leaving only a set of shoe prints on the trunk and a sliding butt print on the roof.

Brown clouds drift from my heels as I hike cross-country. I cover the distance comfortably, humming as I shamble forth, enjoying the hot sunshine on my back. Mom, who monitors my movements more closely now than she did when I was thirteen, thinks I'm seeing a movie and then running errands. I'm not supposed to keep secrets. It's part of this rehab agreement that my every action and decision be approved by Mom and Jane.

With every step I take the house grows larger until it looms right in front of me, bigger and more derelict than

< 15 >

it appears from the road. Every window is coated with layers of grit; shingles are strewn over the ground, flung by some long-ago storm; some of the planks of the balcony are rotted through.

First, the garage. I try each of the three pull-up doors, but they don't budge. I turn the knob on the side door and it opens with a squeak. I'm met by a foul current, a sharp gamey stink that brings tears to my eyes.

A furtive rustle draws the beam of the flashlight upward. It takes a few seconds of adjustment for my mind to comprehend what my eyes are seeing – bats hang from every rafter and cranny. Lowering the light, I gaze at all the guano – so much guano that normal objects are rendered amorphous under its depths. I can't even tell what it is I'm seeing; the mountain in the center might be a car, the hill at the back could be a table, the pyramid in the corner must be a ladder.

I close the door. I'm not squeamish. In fact, I think coming across a real live bat cave is kind of excellent. Certainly more excellent than building a pretend one out of Lego.

I turn my attention to the house.

From what I gathered from the website, urbexers recognize a difference between gaining admittance into an abandoned structure, and breaking and entering – a collective rationalization if ever I've seen one. Nevertheless I'm compelled to at least try to be true to the code, and to that end I'd prefer not to break windows or force locks. The porch feels dry and fragile beneath my heavy boots as I shuffle around, trying every door and window. They're all locked.

But people never lock their upstairs windows and doors.

Donning the gloves, I return to the garage and, making as little noise as possible so as not to disturb, tiptoe in and grab the guano-encrusted ladder.

< 16 >

I brush the filth off its steps, situate it beneath the balcony, and clamber up. After testing the integrity of the iron railing and finding it firm, I pull myself upward, balancing on the edge for only a second before swinging my leg over. I step carefully; the boards aren't in great shape.

The first door I try is unlocked. It opens with a sucking noise, like it's been vacuum sealed. I step inside and close the door behind me.

The first thing I notice is the silence. And the stillness. I don't know that I've ever been in a place so suspended. For several seconds I remain unmoving as I inhale the passage of time.

I seem to have entered through the household office. An ugly desk dominates – an oversized flat surface with no style or craftsmanship to soften its harsh angles. A portrait of a serious-faced man is mounted behind the desk. Judging from the width of the tie and the cut of the lapel, this was painted in the late seventies, early eighties – so this must be Eubert, the last Meskar. The entire room is paneled in dark dull wood, an oppressive decorative trend I've never much cared for. An electric typewriter sits in the middle of the desk. Beside the typewriter is a rotary phone.

A leisurely walk-through of the house takes an hour. Every room is fully furnished. There are six bedrooms, four bathrooms, three full-sized living areas, two dining areas, formal and informal, a game room with a pool table, and a music room with a baby grand piano. The ornaments are lovely and valuable – the lamps are Tiffany, the vases are Waterford, the china in the sideboard is Wedgwood.

Though I find it difficult to believe that I'm the first person to venture here in the last thirty years, the condition of the house tells me this must be so. Every bed is made up.

< 17 >

The flowerpot on the windowsill in the front parlor holds the withered outline of some long-dead plant.

I can also tell that before Eubert Meskar's abrupt departure, he was the only one living here. I arrive at this conclusion because of the few remaining toiletries in the master bathroom – a tube of toothpaste, a cracked and yellowed sliver of soap, a tube of hemorrhoid ointment. None of the other bathrooms have any products at all, only towels stacked in closets. The dishes in the dishwasher tell the same story – one plate, one sauce pan, one glass, one spoon. Here's the story I've heard about why Eubert Meskar left:

He wanted to build an office building on Holt Road, a worthwhile project that would have put money in many pockets, mostly his. But the city planning committee, envious of his wealth and resentful toward his attitude of entitlement, was reluctant to approve it. Several months of bickering followed during which people took sides and enemies were made, until, in a final mean gesture, the committee denied his petition. Enraged, he closed his house and all his businesses – the copper smelter, two car dealerships, three restaurants, four dry cleaners, ten Quik-Stop Marts, and two drive-through beer stops – and left town, taking his money elsewhere and leaving Caprock economically crippled for several years.

I don't know what I expected to get out of this excursion. I'm all alone poking around in the house of a guy who was also all alone. That poor angry man, betrayed by people he thought were his friends; leaving the house he'd lived in all his life. He was a businessman who wanted to do business. What was wrong with that? I wonder where he is now.

I need to be getting home, but I just want to take a quick glance at the attic. Access is through an undersized door

< 18 >

at the end of the second-floor hallway. The narrow stairs squeak in protest as I ascend.

Filtered through the filthy dormers, the light from outside translates into a weak brown haze. Odd pieces of furniture are stored here – an old baby bed, a recliner missing its back, a chest of drawers with no knobs.

Several cardboard boxes form a tower next to the wall on the left. "Winnie" is scrawled on the side of the top box. I've heard about Winona, Eubert's younger sister who died in a car accident in the early seventies. I approach and, lowering the box, rip the dry tape from the top. Pictures, report cards, awards, and certificates – her whole childhood, all neatly stored and saved for posterity. There are a few clothing items which must have been favorites. I shake out a pale blue sweater. It smells musty and the bulky stitches indicate that it's handmade. Beneath the sweater is a doll, still in its original packaging. Behind the plastic is a miniature girl with brown hair, brown eyes, and a frilly pink dress. It's a Chatty Cathy; apparently she says eighteen different things when you pull a string. Why would anyone keep this as one of Winona's cherished possessions when she wasn't even fond enough of it to take it out of the box?

It's time to go. On impulse, I stuff the doll in my backpack, a souvenir of my first urbexing expedition.

The fingerprints left on the few items I've touched are the only indication that I was in the house. I lock the front door from the inside before pulling it closed behind me. Replacing the ladder in the garage, I head toward my car. It was easier to get inside the barbed wire than it is to get out. I have no choice but to crawl under, and I end up with a really nasty six-inch scratch on my back.

< 19 >

Daughters who Disappoint

Jane wears the same kind of boring clothes every day – straight-legged pants with sweater sets in solid colors. Today the pants are navy and the sweater set is a delicate yellow. The fabric across her thighs is stretched to its limits, a reminder that we all have our addictions.

"It's time for you to admit how angry you are with your-self." She says it like it's the first time she's brought it up, but it isn't. These sessions tend to be redundant, which is irritating.

"I'm not."

"Right now you're taking it out on everybody else, but sooner or later you're going to figure out who it is you're really mad at."

"Oh please." I sound like a ten-year-old.

She shifts in her seat and crosses her legs at the knee, drawing attention to her feet in their open-toed sandals. Her feet are like wedges of strawberry cheesecake – smooth and creamy and pink. Her toenails are coral and glossy, cut in the French style, straight across the top with the white edge delineated.

"Anger turned inward can lead to self-destructive behav-ior," she says. "So I think we should discuss how you're going to handle your anger when it hits."

< 20 >

"What kind of self-destructive behavior?" I hope she'll give me some good ideas. But, well trained, she deflects.

"The anger won't go away until you're able to forgive yourself."

"You used to be so fun in high school."

"Tell me about living in New York." She dons an interested expression.

"It's busy," I say, happy to comply. "There's always something to do. You can take a short subway ride and end up in a completely different neighborhood where they speak Chinese or Russian or Arabic or Portuguese. And the way people dress is fascinating – all the cultures shown in fabrics and designs right there on their backs, and you can see how one style influences another. And everybody walks. People are out and moving, not getting from place to place in their solitary cars."

Her eyes have glazed over, which makes me stop talking. The prospect of a world beyond Caprock has rendered her catatonic. It takes her a few seconds to realize I've gone silent.

"Did you use cocaine when you were in New York?" she asks.

"No, that started in Dallas."

"You say 'that started' rather than 'I started.' Why do you think that is?"

"I think I found a possibility for a hobby." She's not the only one who can redirect.

"Oh? Tell me."

"Urban exploration. It's where you go into abandoned buildings or houses and poke around."

"Sounds illegal, so it's out of the question." See? If I'd waited for permission it would never have come. She continues, "But it's fun to think about. I know exactly where

< 21 >

I'd go. The Ramey Building." For an instant her eyes light up the way they used to. Then she deliberately extinguishes her interest, returning to her regular bland and controlled expression.

The Ramey Building. An intriguing possibility. A red brick rectangle eight stories tall, so hideously uninspiring in its construction that it's considered by most to be a blight on the Caprock skyline. It's been through at least four transformations since it was built in the late fifties. First it was a maternity/children's hospital, then a mental institution, then a city offices building. In the early nineties they did a major remodel and it became a jail for several years. When the new jail and courthouse went up on the east side, the doors were locked and the property was fenced in. It's been empty now for at least ten years. There's been talk of tearing it down but so far nothing's come of it. It might make for an interesting excursion. I'll definitely consider it.

"Your parole officer called me to check on your progress," Jane tells me. My affiliation with the Texas legal system is an obscure one. Because I was admitted to the hospital with a drug-induced condition, I was charged with *post facto* possession of an illegal substance. For some reason there's been a delay in transferring my files to Caprock, so I'm still answering to an officer in Dallas, which certainly suits me better than having to check in with someone here once a week. As things stand now, the person overseeing my recovery on the legal end of things is someone I've never even met.

"And did you tell him I was cooperative and cheerful?"

"Of course. Time's up."

I say good-bye and head to my car.

Did you know that people collect Chatty Cathy dolls? Amazing, right? What is it with people who collect stuff?

< 22 >

The doll I took from the Meskar house is apparently a rare model – there weren't as many made with brown hair and eyes as there were blond/blue. And, as the doll has never been out of her packaging, I sold her as "mint" for five hundred dollars. Some woman in Minnesota bought her, sight unseen, without knowing if the speaking mechanism still worked. With my new hobby I'm able to help other people with their hobbies, which is a happy coincidence because Mom said I should help others, and that's exactly what I'm doing.

The surprising success with Chatty Cathy has made me wonder about some of the other items in the Meskar house that have been gathering dust for thirty years. China, crystal, books, albums. I saw on a collectors' website that certain old magazines sell for a hundred an issue – I'm pretty sure I saw some faded National Geographics.

The cashier check for the doll is in my purse. Between Jane's office and home I stop by the bank and open an account that my mother will never know about. It's my little rebellion against my situation, which is absolutely my fault, and my tyrannical mother, who's simply helping with a good heart, like she always does. What will I do with the money? I have no idea. But it makes me feel strong and free, and that's always a good way to feel. The account comes with a debit card and I'm having it delivered to the bank rather than the house. I can pick it up in a week.

When I get home I notice that Mom has posted a little "No Pooping" sign in the middle of the front yard. I enter the house and follow the sound of clattering dishes to the kitchen.

"Hey, you put up a sign," I say, entering and dropping my purse in its allocated spot on the counter. Mom's movements are jerky as she plucks a plate from the dishwasher and flies it

< 23 >

to the overhead cabinet. She's still wearing her work scrubs, pink cotton printed with blue and yellow flowers.

"Where've you been?" Her suspicious scowl accuses me of every misdeed imaginable. "Jane's office said you left forty-five minutes ago."

"You checked up on me? Again? You need to calm down about all this, Mom. I'm an adult. I need some room."

"Talk to me in a year," she says, clearly in a snit.

I open my mouth to argue with her, but the sound of the front door opening shocks us both because, well, each of us is looking at the other person who lives in the house.

"Hello? Anybody home?" It's Chloe, my younger sister. A pre-med student at UT, she's supposed to be doing a summer internship in a research lab in Galveston, so we aren't expecting her home. Mom and I are so thrilled to have a distraction that we race to the front of the house, getting stuck like stooges in the kitchen doorway for a few seconds before exploding into the front room. But we both put on the brakes when we catch sight of Chloe. She's pregnant. Very.

"What the hell?" This from Mom.

"You look like you swallowed your car." This from me.

Chloe pauses in the doorway, as though reluctant to move any further into the house. Her hair flops from an off-center ponytail on top of her head and her feet are bare. She's a cliché. Her abdomen might be huge but the rest of her is as skinny as a feral cat. And her hair, usually golden and glossy, has at least three inches of brown roots showing.

"Surprise!" she says with a weak smile.

Usually we get together at Christmas but this year she said she had to work. Now it's clear what was really going on. I didn't give it much thought at the time; back then the only thing on my mind was my beloved friend, Snow

< 24 >

– where and when I would see him again, and how I could possibly afford him.

"How could you have let this happen?" It's an audacious condemnation from a woman who had two children and has never been married.

Chloe's eyes take on an adversarial gleam. Defiant, she stomps into the living room, leaving her dirty clothes bag in the doorway so the door won't close.

"Like mother like daughter," Chloe says.

"At least I waited until I was out of school. And you girls were planned. You were wanted. You weren't college accidents." True. According to Mom, she carefully selected the fathers of her children – handsome residents, both of them married, neither of them aware they'd fathered us, though their names are right there on the birth certificates. I've always had trouble picturing the actual interactions that led to our conceptions. I imagine she was appealing. The thin neck and big blue eyes give a false impression of fragility; and her full lips always look ready to smile, lending the impression of light-heartedness, also false. But as soon as she speaks anyone can see what she is – strong, independent, and with an unwavering conviction that she's always right. On the other hand, I can see how her sardonic candor would attract. And a hospital is a pool of intense emotions and relationships. But my mother? Sneaking and having sex in the workplace? It's undignified and dishonorable. And the Mom I know is the epitome of poise and integrity. The woman she must have been then – temptress, home wrecker – and the woman she is now – uncompromising, analytical – well, the contrast gives me something to ponder during my wakeful nights.

Mom follows Chloe into the living room, also stomping. I trail along, stunned.

< 25 >

The two face each other, hands on hips, heads thrust forward like belligerent hens. In this air of hostility the blades of the ceiling fan circling over their heads take on a sinister aspect. And self-centered me, I feel a nasty rush of triumph. I'm not the only daughter who disappoints. For the moment at least, Chloe is the naughty sister.

< 26 >

Another Back Porch Night

"It's a sad, sad day when your college daughter comes home pregnant," Mom says.

Zachary and I just nod as Mom takes another gulp of wine. She's already downed a whole bottle and uncorked another. As children Chloe and I gave her no trouble; now that we're grown she's being put through all the agonies she thought she'd managed to escape. She tried to teach us to conduct ourselves sensibly. We're not supposed to become drug addicts or get pregnant before we complete our education. She's not a moralist, but she is adamant about being smart.

We're in the same seats as last night – Mom nearest the door, Zachary facing the house, and me looking out over the back lawn. The light from the kitchen falls on to the porch, lighting up our little area. I'm checking out Jane's Facebook page on my laptop. Her kids are named Doug and Teresa, her husband is Steve, and they went to Paradise Island last summer. There are pictures. Chloe's inside doing her laundry.

"Has she said what her plans are?" Zachary's trying to appear subdued and sympathetic, but he's not fooling us. He loves it when lines are crossed and tempers heat up and accusations fly off tongues like missiles.

Chloe was six years old when I left home. We love each

< 27 >

other but we're not close. I'm more curious about her now than I ever have been. She's always seemed so levelheaded and focused. She makes good grades and lands impressive internships. But getting pregnant and not telling Mom? This is a Chloe I don't know.

"She says she's got a family in line to adopt," Mom tells us. "Do you know why she picked them? Because where they live has one of the best school systems in the country."

This sounds like a good reason to me, but recognizing her frame of mind, I keep my mouth shut. Not so Zachary, who, as I said, likes it when things are stirred up.

"She's thinking about what's best for the child," he says.

Mildly interested, I look up the ranking of public school systems.

"Where is it?" I ask.

"Down around Houston somewhere," Mom says; then, addressing Zachary, "What's best for the child is to stay with its mother. You can't just make a baby and give it away like you would a casserole."

"What are you saying?" he asks. "You think she should keep it?"

"She says she'll be back at school in the fall. Isn't it terrific how everything's going to work out in such a timely manner?" For Mom disillusionment is always a prelude to sarcasm.

"What is it you think she should do?" Zachary shifts and toys with the stem of his glass. "What action could she possibly take that would make you happy at this point?"

"She's talking about Fort Bend County," I tell them. Not relevant, but worth knowing. "It's in the US top hundred. High Asian population."

"What about the father?" Zachary wants to know.

"What about him? They're not together anymore." She

< 28 >

sips and sighs. "I just don't get it. You think you're teaching your kids one thing and it turns out they're learning another."

"Kids learn by example."

"And you know so much about it. I'll pay attention to you when you have kids of your own."

I light a cigarette and Mom shows her disapproval by flapping her hand in front of her face in an attempt to move the smoke along. I gaze sadly at the glowing tip of my cigarette. It's only a matter of time before I'm compelled to give it up. Someday – not tomorrow, but maybe a year from now – I'll be vice-free. Practically perfect. A person with no flaws. How lovely.

"The father should have a say," Zachary persists. "Does he even know she's having his baby?"

"I have no idea," Mom says. "We haven't talked it all out yet."

I change my search to collectibles. An antique table lamp recently sold for six hundred dollars. The one I saw out at the Meskar house was much larger – a domed shade with a wrought iron stand. If the small one is worth six hundred, the floor lamp will definitely be worth more than that.

I type in a search for Eubert Meskar only to find that he died four years ago on his ranch near Bandera. Pulling up a county map to get the description of the Meskar property here in the panhandle, I run the title search only to discover that the land is currently the property of the state. The record refers only to the land. There's no mention of a house. It's possible that the owner – the great state of Texas – is unaware that the house even exists.

"It's a sad, sad day," Mom says again. It seems we've come full circle.

I go in search of my pregnant little sister. She stands at

< 29 >

the counter in the laundry room plucking from a pile of whites, folding, and neatly stacking. The dryer's running. I lean against the jamb and examine her profile. She looks a lot like me – lanky with a narrow jaw and large blue eyes; we both have clear skin, which we got from Mom. She glances up, meets my eye for a second, then returns her attention to her task.

"Did you ever look up your father?" Her question is unexpected. Mom's sperm donors are something we've never talked about.

"Looked him up, sure," I say. "He's got an ENT practice in Irving. Married twice. Three kids from the first marriage."

"So you have three half-siblings that you don't know."

"And I've got one half-sibling that I thought I knew." It's a gentle jab that she chooses to ignore. "A couple of years ago when I got a sinus infection I made an appointment with him, just so I could check him out."

"Wow." Her hands go still. "And?"

"And he's a nice enough guy. Looks like me – tall with blue eyes. I got his hands." My hands are broad and my fingers are long and strong – not delicate or womanly in any way. "He gave me a prescription for an antibiotic."

"Mom's disappointed in me."

"She'll get over it."

"I guess so."

"She's going to pressure you to keep the baby."

"You think?"

"What was going on in your head, Chloe, that you let this happen?" I'm seriously puzzled. With every kind of birth control available at every clinic in Austin, why would a brilliant young woman play so carelessly with her future?

< 30 >

"He was my molecular biology professor," she says. "He's married."

"He could lose his job."

"Yes." The thought seems to make her sad.

"How old is he?"

"Forty-eight."

She's just turned twenty. The picture she's planted in my head makes me shudder.

"If Mom finds out he'll be out on his ass," I say.

"Which is why I'm not going to tell her."

"You want to protect him?"

"If it gets out it'll ruin him. He's got a life. Wife, kids, insurance payments, mortgage. And I knew all that, but I liked him and I flirted and we crossed a line."

"Does he know?"

"I was all over campus looking like this – so he'd be an idiot not to be aware. We'd already decided not to see each other anymore. So we never talked about it."

"When are you due?"

"A couple of weeks."

"I'm sorry about the internship."

"Yeah, me too."

< 31 >

Take Responsibility

By telling Mom I have to be at work at two when I'm really not expected there until three, I've scored myself a free hour to scout the location of my next exploration.

Guarded by a poorly maintained wooden fence, the Ramey Building is in old downtown, a section of Caprock that was run-down when I was a child, but has undergone a dramatic and costly rejuvenation in the last five years. Now, surrounded by trendy shops and themed restaurants, the abandoned building towers like a creepy uncle. I drive around the block several times, unable to get close or get a clear view of the ground floor because of the fence. But I'm near enough to see the long lines of cracks in the mortar and the erosion of the cornerstones. Some of the upper windows are protected by rusty bars, others covered by wired glass, as though, during its stint as a jail, it straddled two eras.

I park on the street and walk across to examine the barrier that's meant to keep people like me out. Many of the planks are warped so badly that nails have actually been pulled from their holes. I add a leveraging tool and ladder to my mental list of supplies.

After formulating a tentative path of entry and determining the best place to park my car, I leave this section of town, heading westward toward a paycheck and several hours of boredom.

< 32 >

This is Zachary's afternoon off, so I'll be spending a couple of overlap hours with the other clerk, Karen, a wife and mother with whom I have nothing in common. The truth is, I find pretty much everything about her to be annoying. Her hair is too yellow and too curly. Her face is so chubby that her glasses rest on her cheeks, not her nose. Her pores are huge and her clothes are uninspiring. But worst of all, she's incapable of carrying on a conversation about anything other than her kids – identical twin girls, thirteen years old.

Ordinarily I'm not this intolerant, but addiction recovery makes me cranky.

Karen's perched on the stool beside the computer when I arrive. Today she wears her gray. She owns four suits, exactly alike in different colors – navy, maroon, gray, and beige. I look over her shoulder. She's registering orders and updating Zachary's deadline calendar.

"Hey, Karen, how's your day going?"

"Holly's got a bit of a sniffle, which of course means Sylvie'll have whatever it is by tomorrow."

"Too bad. How's Gary doing?" Gary's her husband. I know nothing about him other than his name. It's as if, after he impregnated her all those years ago, he ceased to have any place in her life.

"And what is it with teachers and dioramas?" she asks. "One diorama is hard enough, but two is impossible. They should take into consideration that some of us have twins."

"Isn't school out for the summer?"

"This is summer enrichment. A program for gifted children."

"Are ya'll taking a vacation this summer?"

"The girls are just too busy. Tennis camp, science camp, music camp. They're so talented in so many areas. It can be a real problem sometimes."

< 33 >

"I can imagine."

This wouldn't be so mind-numbing if her kids did something interesting every once in a while – like skipping a class or getting caught shoplifting. But she goes on and on and on when there's simply nothing to go on about.

"Do you have a hobby?" I ask.

"My kids take up all my time."

Kids as a hobby. An interesting notion to discuss in therapy.

Mom calls four times that evening to make sure I'm where I'm supposed to be. Karen leaves at seven. Between her departure and closing time, six people wander into the store, none seriously interested in buying diamonds or gold. At a few minutes before nine the phone rings. Thinking it's Mom, my tone is impatient when I answer.

"Olivia?" It's Geraldine, one of my friends from Dallas with whom I'm forbidden to speak.

"God, it's good to hear your voice," I tell her, feeling guilty for breaking the rule, though breaking rules seems to be mainly what I do. "How are you? I miss you so much. How's Vernon doing?"

"We split up. Olivia, I need the money you owe me."

Thirteen hundred dollars. Technically I owe it to both her and Vernon. Eight months ago they helped me make my rent and car payment.

"I do owe you. I know that. But I don't have it." I'm sorry to let her down. Part of rehab is honoring past obligations.

"You promised. I thought I could count on you."

"You can count on me. But you know my situation, right? I can make payments, just like I'm doing with everybody else I owe. I can swing maybe fifty a month."

Even fifty is a stretch. Working part time at minimum wage – it's going to take me years to get out of debt. I

< 34 >

dread Mom's disappointed droop when I tell her that I've got to add another payment to the already long list. I wait for a response from Geraldine, but she terminates the call. My relief is followed by the realization that I'm a horrible person. She was a friend when I needed one. She's obviously in a bind, and all I can think is that now, because she cut me off, I don't have to step up. How depressing. The feeling that I should be better than I am stays with me as I lock up and drive home.

Mom and Chloe are glaring at each other across the kitchen table when I get in. They turn hopeful faces toward me, as though I can offer a solution that'll be acceptable to them both. A half-full glass of milk is in front of Chloe and a yellow legal pad is in front of Mom. She loves her pro/con lists.

"Olivia, tell her I'm right," Mom says. It's both a plea and an order.

"Okay. Chloe, she's right." I'm not sure I believe what I'm endorsing – but what choice do I have? Mom's the boss right now. I pull out a chair and crumple into it, knowing full well that I'm about to be crushed between the two sides of their dispute.

"You don't even know what she's talking about." Chloe looks exhausted. Her face is pinched and her eyes have gray grooves under them. I wonder how long this session's been going on. Mom can be relentless.

"I suppose she's trying to talk you into keeping your baby."

"I live in a cheap apartment with a roommate. I go to school and I work and that's all I do." Obviously that's not all she does; sometimes she has sex. "Taking care of a baby would be impossible."

"Difficult, not impossible." Mom taps the end of her pen against the legal pad.

< 35 >

"Think about it. Childcare, health care, diapers, formula. High chair, stroller, baby bed, clothes. Changing mats, pacifiers, bottles, toys. Do you have any idea what a car seat costs? I can't afford any of it. I had a hundred dollars to spend on groceries last month."

This horrifies me, but Mom seems unimpressed.

"You're twenty, not sixteen. A woman, not a child. It's your baby. Take responsibility."

"I already signed the adoption contract."

"You're not giving away my grandchild."

"I'm going to bed."

Her frustration with Mom is evident in the way she grabs the glass, drains it, slams it back on the table. I feel an affinity; I know what it's like to disappoint Mom. Chloe's thin arms strain as she pushes her front-heavy body from the chair. Mom and I watch her waddle from the room. A hundred dollars. About three dollars a day. No wonder she's so skinny.

"The way her belly pokes out looks painful." I rub my flat tummy sympathetically.

"What do you think about this, Olivia? How can I just let it go?" She believes a mother takes care of her children. It's a code she's lived by. It's a code she expects us to live by.

"Why do you think she waited until now to come home?" This has been nagging at me – why now? Why not six months ago? Or better yet – why come home at all? She had to have known what Mom's reaction would be.

"Because she wants to be talked out of giving her baby away." Mom always speaks with such conviction. No second-guessing, no self-doubt.

"Maybe she's scared. Maybe she just wants her mother." When life turns overwhelming, the place I most want to be is hunkering in the protection of my mother's shadow. She

< 36 >

may gripe and she may have impossible expectations, but she loves me and she's the strongest person I know. That doesn't mean she's not hard to take. Her authoritative voice can rankle.

"So you're on her side."

"I'm empathizing with her. If she keeps this child she'll have to give up her dream. It really would be impossible for her to go to med school and care for a baby."

"Life means doing what needs to be done as you move forward." She issues this sentence as though it's an established and indisputable philosophy. "You're okay with your niece or nephew being raised by strangers?"

"I honestly haven't thought about it." It's Chloe's predicament, not mine. I have enough to do taking care of myself.

"When will you think about it, Olivia? This is a major family issue – so tell me, when will you get over yourself and have an opinion about anything other than how the universe has done you wrong?"

So now it's my turn to be the target of her wrath. I'm not going to argue with her. She goes on for several minutes, listing the ways I've failed, mourning my lost career, berating my current apathetic attitude. Her diatribe washes over me as I allow my shoulder and neck muscles to relax and my eyes to glaze over. I hang on to thoughts of the night ahead, my next adventure.

After a while she winds down.

"You're not going to fix us tonight," I tell her.

It's ten-fifteen and she has to be up in the morning for the seven-to-three shift. I've never seen her look so weary. I guess in one way she's right – I've been so self-absorbed these last few weeks that I'm just now noticing how much smaller she is than she used to be. And she's faded, too.

< 37 >

Her golden hair has turned silver and her blue eyes, once a brilliant lapis, are now more the color of bleached denim.

She heads toward her bedroom on the other side of the living room, and I head toward mine, which is across the front of the house, up the stairs, at the end of the hall. We turn out lights and lock doors as we go.

< 38 >

Chloe Comes Along

The light is on in Chloe's room. I tap and enter. Resting her back against the headboard, she wiggles like she's having a hard time finding a comfortable position. Her room, unlike mine, is exactly as she left it three years ago when she went to college. In cheerful hues of pink and yellow, it's in contrast to her purple-bruised mood. My room was unchanged, too, during my college years. But as soon as I moved to New York, Mom collected the posters from the walls, boxed up the high school memorabilia, and lugged in her exercise bike and sewing machine. At least she left my bed.

"Hey," Chloe says, gazing mournfully at her toes. "I haven't been able to reach my feet for weeks."

"You could use a pedicure." I can't help but compare her dry scraggly toenails to Jane's glossy ones.

"Foot care is the first thing to go when you don't have money."

"Tell me about it."

I, too, have had to sacrifice professional pedicures, but at least I can reach my feet to see to their upkeep. We sigh in unison. Poor Chloe. Lack of money is the curse of most college students. I remember it well. What I didn't get in scholarship and grant money, Mom paid. Tuition was high when I was in school, and costs have gone up dramatically since. And though Mom bought both of us cars

< 39 >

when we graduated from high school, she didn't pay for gas, insurance, or maintenance. And when we moved from the dorms, she paid our monthly rent, but she didn't pay for food or clothes or extra-curriculars. And costs pile up. For instance, considering Chloe's current expenses, it costs two hundred and seventy dollars to take the MCAT – and in addition, there's an eighty-five dollar processing fee for every copy of her test scores forwarded to the schools where she's applying.

"Hey," I say, moving into the room and propping a hip on the edge of the mattress. "You want to hear about a fun thing to do in Caprock?"

"Sure."

I tell her about going into the Meskar Mansion, about how the hike from the side road was long and hot, and how the old-style furniture and appliances evoked visions of another era. It's gratifying to see how the notion of exploring the old house cheers her. All her worries seem to fall away as her eyes light up. But the pleasure I get from entertaining her crashes when, after I tell her that my next excursion will be tonight and that I'm going into the Ramey Building, she insists on coming.

"No way," I tell her. "You're in no condition to be traipsing through God-knows-what'll be in there."

"I'll be really, really careful. Anyway, it's a solid building, not a falling-down ruin. There won't be anything to it other than walking up and down some stairs with a flashlight."

"You'll slow me down."

"I won't, I promise. And so what if I do? It's not a race."

I'm dubious. But she's always had the most compelling pout. She's my baby sister and I can't say no to her. Also, I admit, it would be nice to have some company. I've been lonely.

< 40 >

"Okay. But I'm not leaving here until one-thirty." Hopefully she'll fall asleep before then and this whole discussion will be proved pointless.

I make my way to my own bed and set the alarm for one-fifteen. But one of the side effects of the pills is insomnia; my restless doze can hardly be called sleep. I get up ten minutes before the alarm goes off. Donning my clothes and boots and grabbing my backpack, I head toward Chloe's room. She opens the door before I reach it.

"I thought you'd be asleep," I tell her, disappointed that she's still awake.

"I'm too uncomfortable to sleep." Wearing jeans and hiking boots, she grins and holds her flashlight aloft.

We sneak out of the house. Remembering that I want to take some tools, we stop by the garage and get the fold-out ladder, a hammer, and a screwdriver. The ladder won't fit in the trunk so I slide it across the back seat, opening the rear driver's-side window so that it protrudes by at least a foot.

The new businesses around the Ramey Building include a couple of bars, which are just closing. A few tail-lights disappear in the distance – drinkers heading home to their beds. Nostalgia slips over me. I used to stay at the bars until closing. I wasn't fond of alcohol; in fact, I could spend the entire night sipping on one glass of white wine. My substance of choice wasn't poured at the bar; it was snorted in the bathroom.

I take the first right, then the next right into the alley, pulling deep into the shadow of Berto's, a Tex-Mex restaurant that, though it's been closed for hours, still emits the warm aromas of tortillas and refried beans. In an effort to conceal the car, I park on the blind side of the dumpster, squeezing as close to the wall as possible. Chloe's forced to extricate herself by bumping her backside over the console,

< 41 >

squeezing her gigantic tummy beneath the steering wheel, and exiting from the driver's side – a process which includes lots of grunting and huffing. Already she's slowing me down. We fetch our gear and, emerging cautiously from the protection of the alley, cross the street in silence.

I choose a couple of planks where the bottom nails are already pulled loose because of the extreme warping. Opening and climbing the ladder to gain access to the top, I insert the lever-end of the hammer and remove the top nails. They all slide out with only a slight effort and a rusty squeak. I lower the planks as I free them, leaning them against the fence. Getting inside the perimeter goes pretty much as planned – except instead of removing two planks I have to remove three because of Chloe's girth. I fold the ladder, pull it in after us, and turn to look up at the building, which, from this vantage, appears dauntingly impenetrable. Beyond the silhouette of the looming fortress the moon is bright silver; pale clouds make delicate waves across the sky. I inhale the night air. All is utterly, perfectly, silent.

"How do we get in?" she whispers.

"We circle and look for the easiest access." I, too, am whispering.

"It looks way sinister."

"Yeah."

I've never been led by my imagination and I've certainly never been frightened by the dark, but the wall in front of me seems alive with drifting shapes; and the windows, which offered a dull reflection during the daylight hours, now appear to be black mouths ready to gobble us up.

Starting at the side of the building, we circle right, toward the front, searching for an entry point. The structure is split at ground level. The window wells a few feet beneath us offer possible access, as do the windows several

< 42 >

feet above our heads. I scramble down and try the lower windows while Chloe situates the legs of the ladder, scales awkwardly, and tries the upper windows. On the ninth try, near the front of the building, I get lucky. The latch on one of the windows has a little give to it. I yank it a couple of times and jimmy it with the screwdriver. The window jiggles a little bit more with every wrench until it jerks free.

"I got it," I whisper-call to Chloe.

The rails of the frame are misshapen and full of grit, so the upward movement of the window is uneven and laborious. I make a mental note to add a can of WD-40 to my supplies.

Chloe climbs down the ladder, folds it, and drags it to my little well, where I'm hunched down and peering in. The flashlight beam casts odd shapes in the room below – extensive partitioning of some kind. An unfinished ceiling is crossed by pipes that create plaid shadows.

"I'm going in." I toss my backpack in and slip through on my stomach, feet first. Wiggling through the opening I dangle for a few seconds before letting go. I drop a couple of feet and land easily. Chloe'll never be able to get down here like that.

I shine the light all around. What looked like partitions turns out to be rows and rows of metal shelving. This must have been used as a library, or a storage area of some sort. The air is stagnant and cool and the only odor is that of stale dust.

"This window's awfully small." Chloe's voice is thin and fearful. I have no idea how she worked herself into the tight space, but it can't have been pretty. I turn my attention toward getting her down here.

"Maybe you should go back to the car." It's a reasonable suggestion.

< 43 >

"I'm pretty sure I can squeeze through. But how'll I get down?"

"Lower the ladder," I tell her.

She has to clamber out of the well to get the ladder. With a few metallic knocks and rattles, the legs of the ladder poke at me from above. I lower it, open its legs, and adjust it below the window. She grunts as she climbs down and squats.

"Okay, sit on your butt and slide through. I'll guide your feet."

I climb the bottom step of the ladder and reach up, prepared to grasp her feet. But her feet come to a halt when they're about a foot above the top rung.

"I'm stuck," she tells me, sounding far away.

Stepping off the ladder and aiming the beam upward, I get a clear view of her huge belly caught on the lower edge of the upper window. A meta moment; coming through the opening like that, it looks like she's being given birth to – but this is no time to indulge in weird fantasies. Her rear end sags just below the sill and her legs and feet are suspended. That's got to be uncomfortable – unsafe, too. I climb the ladder, grab her feet, and manage to push her back up a few inches so that at least her bottom is supported. This is absurd. I take a second to ask myself the question I seem to be asking a lot lately – what the hell was I thinking?

"Try turning sideways. The window is wider than it is high."

Her suspended feet kick as she tries to turn her belly to the side. She manages to free her baby bump and her feet once again begin to descend. I take hold of her ankles and place her feet on the top rung. Once her feet are on the solid surface the rest of her emerges. She straightens and,

< 44 >

holding on to the sill for balance, looks down at me from beyond the hump of her stomach.

"How great is this?" she asks.

How are we going to get her out of here? She can hardly get out the way she came in.

< 45 >

Unexpected Findings

With both flashlight beams scanning, we work our way around the edge of the rows of shelves, staying close to the wall. My expectations are vague – I guess I just want to see what's in here. I cannot imagine that the old building holds secrets – or, for that matter, anything more interesting than a couple of hundred empty rooms. But here I am, pleased to be walking through it.

"What do we do first?" she asks.

"Let's find the stairs and go up."

"Why are we whispering?"

"Because we're sneaking and sneaky people whisper."

We come to a door. It offers a small window at eye level and I shine my light in at all the equipment necessary to support a building this size – massive heater and AC units, fuse boxes, generator, etc. We move on. The next door leads to a set of cement steps. The handle turns easily, the heavy door creaks, and we're on our way to the main floor.

I explained the rules of urbexing to Chloe on the way over. The object, I told her, is to leave as little evidence of our presence as possible. No touching, no damaging. The fun is in imagining the history. Our goal is not to disturb, but to explore and learn – even so, the stairs are coated with dust and we both leave distinct footprints. See, that's the

< 46 >

inherent paradox of the code – no matter how careful we are, a record of our presence is inevitable.

The first floor was used for administration in every one of the building's incarnations. Shoulder-to-shoulder, we tromp through, assigning locations for the various tasks that would have been performed. The pedestal beside the front door would have served as a vantage point for a security guard; and the long counter that stretches across the back of the foyer – reception and information. The front door is impressive – double frame, dark wood with intricately carved trim, at least twelve feet high; it reminds us that this structure housed a well-funded enterprise at one time. The floor is marble with a center mosaic of the Texas Lone Star. Spaced evenly along the wall, wires protrude like ragged appendages where the sconces have been removed – also from the ceiling where a central chandelier once hung.

Behind the counter two hallways reach toward the back of the building. From this angle, in this darkness, it's impossible to determine how far they extend. We take the hallway on the right, shining our lights in each doorway, giving a few seconds of inspection to each room. Offices, no furniture, no old file cabinets, no pictures.

"Are we the first people in here since it was locked up?" asks Chloe. "How many years ago was that?"

"About ten, I think."

"And in all that time no one's done what we're doing now?"

"The people of Caprock are not known for their adventurous spirits."

We're nearing the rear of the building, getting close to where we removed the planks from the fence. Entering the next office, I cross to the window, unlatch it, and slide it open. The drop to the ground is less than five feet. If I help

< 47 >

Chloe lower herself from the sill, the drop will only be a couple of feet. This'll be her exit.

"Let's keep going up." I plan to cover every one of the eight floors.

We return to the stairs and trudge upward, but we're taken by surprise on the next floor.

The layout is the same – offices at the rear and a larger room at the front. So far, from what we've seen, the building was stripped before it was vacated – so to find mountains of architectural fixtures stored in the front room is unexpected. From one side of the room to the other, every inch of floor is covered except for a yard-wide aisle through the center.

We pass our beams over doors, windows, stacks of wood. Toilets and sinks. I scan the open boxes at my feet – several of them, full of old doorknobs. Quite old doorknobs, in fact. I pluck one and hold it to the light. It's delicate, cut glass.

"Antique," I say.

Beyond the knobs is a row of iron grates, intricately molded ventilation covers of a type that hasn't been in use since the mid-nineteen hundreds. I slip the doorknob into my pocket and pick up one of the vent covers. It's cold in my hands, and so dirty that I can feel the grit. Substantial, elegant, and built to last forever. It makes me sad for all the lovely things we've let slip away. The intake covers in our house are cheap, lightweight, and without style. Why can't something utilitarian also be beautiful?

I hold on to it, reluctant to put it down. A sign reading "Kiowa" draws my attention. Scripted in big black letters, it's propped against the far wall.

"Look," I say, nodding toward the sign. "All this stuff's from the Kiowa Hotel."

< 48 >

Erected in the late eighteen hundreds, the Kiowa played a notable role in the formation of our small city. For a period of at least ten years it was the only hotel for three hundred miles in any direction. Old pictures show it to be a grand building with balconies overlooking what was then called Main Street (renamed Roosevelt Avenue in the sixties) and swinging doors like they have in cowboy films. It closed down in the middle of the century until, after standing empty for decades and enduring years and years of dry wind and harsh sun, the city commission decided it was time to call in the demolition crew.

"They just stuck all these old bits and pieces in here?"

"Looks like it." I replace the grate. I wonder who owns all these fixtures.

We march upward. The third floor holds the court-rooms; they've been stripped bare, which I take as a signal that there'll probably be no more surprises.

The jail portion of the building starts on the fourth floor. Historically, incarceration in Caprock is a joint venture. Because Caprock is situated at the juncture of three counties and is the official seat for these counties, it facilitates both the city jail and a tri-county jail, along with the legal branches of all four governmental bodies. Caprock alone wouldn't need more than thirty or so cells to accommodate its local miscreants – but throw in all the area and small towns in a hundred mile radius, and the need for space multiplies radically.

A metal detector and a booth enclosed in bullet-proof glass signal our entry to the jail. Both are criss-crossed by spider webs weighted by years of dust. When we walk through they cling to us. A massive industrial kitchen opens to our right; we illuminate it briefly – all stainless steel, even the counters and shelving. It's been stripped – no

< 49 >

utensils, pots and pans, or appliances; even the faucets have been removed. Next we come to an open area – most likely the cafeteria. Beyond this is another big room – a gym or a recreation hall.

We don't see cells until we arrive at the fifth floor. The walls that divide the units are solid, but each is fronted by heavy bars. Nothing has been dismantled. Two silver bowls are mounted on the walls of each cell – a toilet and a sink. Cot racks are bracketed to walls – one bed per cell. We're getting a clear picture of life in the loser lane. It's pretty depressing.

"This is so bizarre that we're doing this," Chloe says.

I know what she means. Our beams playing across the bars form dancing stripes. Other than our soft footsteps there is an absolute lack of sound. And the stink of defeat that should have faded years ago still hangs in the air, evoking thoughts of failures, bad decisions, and delusions. How many of the people who slept in these cells were addicts?

"You alright?" I ask after we climb another set of stairs. She seems out of breath. We shuffle along. Sixth floor, more of the same.

"Getting sleepy."

It's almost four a.m. We need to be going soon. Mom gets up at a quarter to six.

"Let's keep going. We've got time." Okay, so I'm goal-obsessed. I wanted to do all floors and that's what I intend to do. What kind of exploration is it if you don't explore the whole thing?

We find the remains of a dead guy on the seventh floor.

"What's that?" Chloe asks, shining her light into one of the cells. At first all we can tell is that it's a shadowy lump in the furthest corner. But as both our beams highlight the

< 50 >

shape, it becomes very obviously skeletal. Chloe emits a shriek and clutches my arm.

"Wow," I tell her. "You found a dead body." I'm not prone to extreme reactions these days, a result of anti-depressants and beta blockers.

"I didn't find it. You found it." Her voice has gone squeaky with panicked terror. She's squeezing my arm so hard that there'll be bruises.

It grins with huge teeth, the way skeletons do. At this time of night, in this eerie light, it seems surreal, more parody than actuality, hardly horrible or horrifying at all. Stringy blond hair pokes out from beneath a baseball cap. The reason I think it's a guy is because the shoes are large.

"How long do you think he's been here?" I ask, hoping my lack of excitement will calm her, which it does.

"No idea." Her near-hysteria has been replaced by pragmatic assessment.

"Look at what he's wearing," I say, and she focuses her light on the logo on the left side – golden arches.

"Is that a McDonald's uniform?"

"Looks like. One of the older ones. So he's been here a while."

"Any evidence of foul play?" She's seen too many cop shows.

"I doubt he came to this out-of-the-way place to expire from natural causes."

"This isn't the kind of thing you stumble across every day."

"No."

"We have to tell someone."

"If we do, we'll have to admit we were here." My first reaction in most circumstances these days is to admit nothing and stay out of the light.

"We could call in an anonymous tip."

< 51 >

"Maybe."

Could they trace it to us? How deep would an investigation go? We're talking about a body, so yeah, pretty deep. Would police look for evidence in this single cell or would they go over the whole building? We've left footprints, but very few fingerprints.

"This has totally creeped me out," she says with a shudder. "Let's get out of here."

Five minutes later I'm helping Chloe out the first-floor office window. She lowers herself through, no problem. I latch the window behind her, wipe it with my T-shirt because now I'm paranoid about leaving prints, and head toward the basement – but the weight of the doorknob in my pocket reminds me of the iron grates on the second floor, and I realize that I've got to have one of those, too. So I take a quick run up the stairs and grab the vent cover.

My exit is a reversal of my entrance. In the basement I climb the ladder, lift and slide the heavy grille through the window, scramble up and out, and, reaching down, pull the ladder behind me. This latch, too, I wipe with the tail of my shirt. Then I clamber out and around to the back of the building, replace the planks in the fence, and we're done.

At home Chloe rushes inside because apparently her bladder is now the size of a peanut. I put the ladder back in the garage and enter the house through the back door. I'm just dozing off when I hear Mom stirring downstairs.

< 52 >

Support Group

As part of addiction recovery I'm required to participate in a support group. The meetings are held on Thursday evenings, seven-thirty, in the upstairs parlor of the education building of St. John's Methodist Church. Because there are few addicts in Caprock, we combine all addictions for one weekly meeting. Gambling, alcohol, laxatives, Vicodin – if it can be abused someone among us has abused it. Anybody who does anything to excess is welcome. We have one woman who spends two hours a day in a tanning bed, another who chews on her hair.

I'm sitting next to Sue, my sponsor. When it came to selecting the person to guide me through this stretch of recovery, I chose the person who seemed least likely to stick her nose in. A mild woman in her sixties, she comes to meetings because twenty years ago, for a short amount of time, she grew dependent on valium. She knits as she listens to people's testimonies. It gets her out of the house.

The coffee and cookies are provided by the church women – and Methodist women are competitive when baking is involved. They bring in plates towering with oatmeal and raisin cookies that dissolve on your tongue. The chocolate chip cookies are so fresh that the chocolate's still hot and syrupy. Peanut butter, macaroons, chocolate

< 53 >

hazelnut, vanilla marshmallow, orange ginger – circles of magic, a whole new addiction category.

Tonight a lumpish man with a red face is telling about how he hasn't had a drink in seven years, but sometimes he wants one. Seven years. Shouldn't these people move on? It can't be healthy to dwell on the part of your life when things went horribly wrong. Will I have moved on in seven years? Or will I still yearn for my precious coca the way this man longs for his drink?

"I drink coffee or water or juice," he tells us, "but it doesn't satisfy, not the way alcohol satisfies. I miss the way alcohol burns my throat and then warms me all over so that I feel like nothing bad in the world will ever touch me. But I turn away from it because it took everything from me – my family, my career, my self-respect. I just can't let myself go there again."

"Praise the Lord," Sue intones like she does every time someone stands strong against temptation. *Click, click* go her knitting needles.

I'm pretty sure the body in the cell was Johnny Kessler, eighteen years old, who went missing six years ago. I found his description on a website for missing people in Texas. High school student, drummer in the school marching band, part time McDonald's employee, beloved son and brother. That means that his body was there when the workmen transferred the fixtures from the Kiowa Hotel to the Ramey Building. The only way to find out how he died or what led him to that place is to report his body to the police and let them sort it out, which is probably what we're going to do. I know Chloe wants to, but she seems to be awaiting sanction from me. She thinks the family deserves closure, and I know she's right. I appreciate her giving me time. I'm slow these days; it takes a while for things to sink in.

"Your bag is buzzing," Sue says.

< 54 >

The woman in front of me – Cam, addicted to chili fries – turns and gives me a look. We're supposed to turn off our phones before we come into the room. I reach into the side pocket of my purse and pull out my vibrating phone. It's an area code I don't recognize. Risking mass disapproval, I take it out to the hallway.

"Hello?"

"Are you the person who has antique fixtures for sale?" It's a woman, accent Pacific Northwest.

"I only have a vent cover and a crystal doorknob."

"And they're in good condition?"

"Yes."

"Can you provide more?"

Can I? Maybe. I suppose.

"I'll make you a good offer."

"I've already had three calls." This surprises me. Who are these people and why do they want a vent cover and a doorknob?

"And what about other fixtures?" she asks. "Hinges or switch plates?"

"Yes, I think so." I vaguely recall catching sight of a carton of smaller items.

"A hundred per grate, fifty per knob," she offers. "And for switch plates and hinges, with corresponding screws, I'll pay twenty-five a set."

This is the exact same amount the other callers have offered, except they made no mention of hinges or switch covers. These people must be getting their price information from the same source, which means it is what it is. Time to commit.

"Okay. I'll see what I can do and I'll get back to you in a day or two." It looks like I'm going back into the Ramey Building.

< 55 >

When I get home Mom's gone to bed. Though the sky is clear, the moon is tiny and distant, which makes the world seem darker than usual. Zachary and Chloe are no more than murmuring shadows on the back patio. Zachary's sipping wine and Chloe's drinking vitamin water. I go inside, grab a water from the refrigerator, and come back out.

"What are we talking about?" I ask, joining them and lighting a cigarette. The distant twinkle of the stars makes me feel at peace. Nothing is moving – not the clouds, not the tree branches; even the cicadas are quiet. "What a beautiful night."

"Inspirational," Zachary agrees.

"How was group?" Chloe asks. She and I need to talk – how do I tell her not to make her anonymous call until tomorrow without telling her why?

"We got a new member who's addicted to Spider Solitaire. Ten hours a day, seven days a week. She takes breaks to do what she has to do to live her life, then she returns to her game. What started as a mindless pastime became an addiction. Doesn't anybody have control of themselves?" My own voice comes to me as though I'm speaking from far away.

"Zachary's having his say about the baby," Chloe tells me.

"Oh? So what do you think, Zachary?"

"I think giving her baby away is going to be harder than she thinks. I think that once she gives birth to it she'll never be able to let it go." As always, he's coming down firmly on Mom's side. Chloe doesn't seem to mind that he's talking about her in the third person. "I also think she could do both."

"Med school and single motherhood?" she asks. "It'd be impossible." I agree.

< 56 >

"You're young," he says. "So what if you go a few years without sleep? It'd be worth it – you'd come out of it with a child and a medical degree."

"But I've signed the contract."

"It's not binding. No one on the planet can force you to give your baby away."

"He's right," I surprise myself by chiming in. I honestly thought I had no opinion on the subject – but Mom was right. Someone else raising my niece or nephew doesn't feel right.

"But I'm so poor," Chloe whines.

"Maybe you're not as poor as you think," he says. "There's one option you haven't explored."

He scoots his chair back, stands, and gives a groan as he stretches. With a "take your ease, chickadees" he saunters off, disappearing through the back gate.

"What's he talking about?" she asks.

"Have you ever looked up your biological father?"

"You're saying I should ask some stranger to help me out just because he had sex with my mother twenty years ago?"

I let her question hang. As ideas go, this could be a very good one or a very bad one.

"Do you know what Mom told me once?" she asks. "She said the reason she had me was because she loved you so much."

"Every person I knew in high school is married with kids. Caprock. Where individuality goes to die."

"No matter what you tell yourself, individuality and addiction are not synonymous."

"Hey, I can euphemize with the best of them."

"The body was Johnny Kessler. He disappeared six years ago."

"I looked him up, too. One of us should call it in

< 57 >

tomorrow. You do it." I have no desire to instigate contact, even anonymously, with the local cops.

"He's a dermatologist in Aimes." Back to her biological father. "Other than that, I know nothing about him."

"It'd be easy enough to find out." Aimes is a small town about an hour north of Caprock. If I've ever been there I don't recall it.

"What time do you have to be at work tomorrow?"

"Not until five." She wants me to go spying with her. I can do that. "But I need to catch up on my sleep – let's not leave until around eleven."

She goes to bed. I'm exhausted, but know that if I go to bed I'll just lie there, longing for a sleep that won't come and counting the minutes until I can reasonably kick back the covers and go. So I watch *The Maltese Falcon* on the classics channel. As soon as the end credits start, I turn off the TV and take my stealthy leave.

Two hours later I return. The trunk of my car is weighed down with a dozen heavy grates, twenty knob sets, and a box of switch plates and hinges – with matching screws. It took me four trips into the building to haul it all out. I took everything small enough to carry. The remaining items are too big – toilets, sinks, even a set of saloon doors. In a few days I will be able to add approximately twenty-five hundred to my covert account.

< 58 >

Hard Being You

The first thing that comes to mind when someone thinks about addiction recovery is the twelve-step program, which is a misnomer because there are only six steps, though in the 1939 version there were twelve. Of the original twelve, six of them are geared toward having a relationship with God – seeking, believing, confessing, petitioning, submitting. These days the God clauses have been condensed into one all-encompassing statement which simply requires recognition of a "Higher Power" – and the way it's worded, the higher power can be whatever or whoever I want it to be. I can pray to a chair if the whim takes me.

So in an attempt to adhere to the program, Jane insists that I spend fifteen minutes every morning meditating about what God means to me and what He can do in my life.

"I don't mean lying in bed in the morning with your eyes closed," she said, "all cozy beneath the covers while you let your mind drift and tell yourself you're thinking about God." She introduced this topic during our first session. I remember feeling belligerent at the time – toward her and her spruced-up family staring out of the photo, and toward the God she wanted me to ponder. "I'm talking about getting out of bed, reading a passage of something spiritual, and truly sharing yourself with a superior being."

< 59 >

Because I have a Protestant background, I'm most comfortable sticking with Christian doctrine – though, in my experience trying to communicate with any aspect of the Trinity is a waste of time. But because I really do want to get my life back, I comply. Before I have coffee, before I open my door, I get out of bed and sit in a straight-backed chair – straight-backed because Jane seems to think being comfortable isn't conducive to prayerful contemplation – and open the Bible that was a gift from the Baptist Sunday school when I was in third grade. I alternate daily between the old covenant and the new, the obdurate God and the merciful one. Today is a New Testament day and the Bible falls open at the book of Jude, which is unlikely because, considering the magnitude of the tome, Jude is only two pages long. Jude verses 11–13 – here it is:

Woe to them! For they have gone the way of Cain, and for pay they have rushed headlong into the error of Balaam, and perished in the rebellion of Korah. These are the men who are hidden reefs in your love feasts when they feast with you without fear, caring for themselves; clouds without water, carried along by winds; autumn trees without fruit, doubly dead, uprooted; wild waves of the sea, casting up their own shame like foam; wandering stars, for whom the black darkness has been reserved forever.

Quite the rant. The error of Balaam? Hidden reefs in your love feasts? Talk about your mixed metaphors. The writer in me appreciates the images of the descriptive section – clouds without water, doubly dead, casting up shame like foam. An evocative way with language, this Jude. But how can I apply this to my life, how is this useful to me? I close my eyes, empty my mind, and wait for God's voice, which people have described to me as soft and coming from a great distance, and which I myself have never heard. In the end

< 60 >

God doesn't speak and I have to rely on my own interpretation. Here's what I get out of the passage: pursue worthy goals, don't be a hidden reef, and exercise self-control – and if I act shamefully, producing nothing, I'll end up in the black darkness that has been reserved for me forever.

Okay, I'll try. I already have a daily goal, which is to get through the day without Blanca, my friend who enticed me, broke me, and then deserted me. As for self-control, how else am I going to meet my daily goal? And as far as being productive is concerned, I'm going to spend a good portion of the day helping my sister stalk her father – an undeniable act of generosity.

There's a tap on my door and Chloe pops her head in.

"Mom gave me gas money," she says, waving two twenties. She comes in the room, sits on the bed, and plops backward so that her stomach pokes up like a mountain.

"You told her where we were going and why?"

"No. I just told her we were hanging out. She says she needs to know where you are at all times."

"She takes this custodial crap way too seriously."

"We got some role reversal going on. You used to babysit me and today I'm babysitting you." She waves the money again. "She thinks if she bribes me she'll get what she wants."

"It's not what she wants – it's what she wants for you."

"Why are you taking her side?"

I sigh and close the Bible.

"Is that helping?" She nods toward the Bible.

"It gives me something to think about besides blow."

"Then you must really like having me here. I'm quite the distraction these days."

"That you are."

"I had breakfast with Mom at the hospital this morning

< 61 >

and I called about Johnny's body from there – they have a thousand landlines so it'll be impossible to trace."

Okay. Good. I'm glad I got the stuff I needed last night.

"I bet it's on the news by noon." She's excited by her small part.

Fifteen minutes later I'm sipping coffee, sucking yogurt off a spoon, and researching the Kiowa Hotel to see who owns the fixtures I just took from the Ramey Building. Just like the Meskar property, the lot the Kiowa occupied belongs to the great State of Texas. There's no mention of the removed fixtures at all. The state doesn't own the building in which the fixtures are stored; the Ramey Building is owned by the city. I'm getting a picture here – local and state governments unwieldy and unaware, not in communication with one another. Assets undiscovered and undocumented. Curious, I check to see what other derelict properties in the area are in the hands of the government. Within a two-hour radius of Caprock, I find schools, churches, gas stations. And here's something interesting – there's an old drive-in movie theater thirty miles north of here, conveniently halfway between here and Aimes, listed as property of the state.

Chloe's baby-belly enters the kitchen; and then the rest of her arrives. She's ready to hit the road, so I put my yogurt spoon in the dishwasher, the empty container in the trash, and follow her to her car. It doesn't take long to get out of town. The two-lane highway is busier than I thought it would be. All it does is go north as far as Liberal – why are all these people going in that direction?

"Can I ask you something?" I ask. When she was six and I was eighteen, I took her everywhere with me. She was cheerful and she adored me. It's gratifying to have someone adore you simply because you exist. But that was then. I don't really know the woman she's become.

< 62 >

"Sure."

"Do you really want to go to medical school?"

"Being in therapy doesn't make you a therapist."

"I may not be a therapist, but I recognize self-sabotage when I see it."

"You're one to preach about self-sabotage."

The implication is irritating. I've spent the last few months trying to convince every counselor on my recovery agenda that I didn't turn to drugs because I wanted to escape my life. It's simply not true. I loved my life. I loved my job. The addiction just happened. And it won't happen again – and predictably, irrationally, this unfounded faith in my own strength infuses me with a longing for cocaine that steals my breath and invades my mind. I inhale deeply, holding the air in my lungs, as I mentally beat it back.

"This isn't about me," I tell her. "It's about you and how maybe this accident of yours wasn't an accident as much as it was an attempt to get off the path you were on. Changing direction at your age is normal."

"If I wanted to get out of going to medical school I wouldn't be putting the baby up for adoption."

"Mom thinks you came home to be talked out of it."

"What do you think my father'll look like?"

"Exactly like you. Short, fat, bald, near-sighted with a hooked nose, and chubby cheeks." I've been keeping an eye out for the entrance to the old drive-in. It's coming up on the right. "On the way back I'm going to want you to turn in there so we can check out that abandoned drive-in."

There's a dilapidated sign on the verge. The words "High Plains Drive-in Theater" are so faded that they're barely legible. An arrow points to the east, down a bumpy road that's overgrown with weeds. The top of the gigantic screen

< 63 >

is visible from the highway. From this distance it looks lop-sided and ragged.

"Maybe your life was too easy," I say. "Maybe you weren't feeling challenged, so you thought you'd stir things up, make things harder."

She snorts.

"It's not as silly as it sounds. People build their own stumbling blocks all the time."

"You want the truth? I don't know what I want. I don't know why I came home. I don't know if I want to go to medical school. I don't know why I slept with a professor. I don't know any of it."

"It's hard being you right now."

"It's hard being you, too."

We both smile, united in our misery.

Aimes is a flat colorless town laid out in an unimagina-tive grid. In an attempt to put off what we came here to do, Chloe takes a right at the Dairy Queen. We drive up and down residential streets. The lots are big, each with a scrawny elm and patchy grass for landscaping. The houses are at least forty years old, brick, and one-storey; most have car ports instead of garages. Occasionally there's a bike or wagon in the driveway or a swing and slide in the yard. Who lives here? Where do they work and what do they do? Eventually she runs out of houses to gawk at and we end up at the Wal-Mart, which must be where everyone from the surrounding area congregates because the parking lot is packed. There are at least fifty people pushing shopping carts between the store and their cars. Our destination is the brick building across the street. The large sign by the curb reads "Aimes Medical Tower", a grand designation for an edifice of only four stories. Chloe crosses at the intersec-tion, pulls around the building and into a parking place,

< 64 >

turns off the car, and then just sits there. Determined to let her have all the time she needs, I get out of the car and, leaning against the front right fender, indulge in a cigarette. The highway runs right through the town, and though we're a quarter of a mile away, the sound of traffic is constant. A hot dry wind carries my smoke toward Oklahoma. The view in front of the car is a weedy lot. When I finish my cigarette I stomp it out in the gutter and get back in the car. It's like sinking into an oven. I try to close my eyes and doze, but my eyes never stay closed for long these days.

"Well?" I finally ask, losing patience as sweat begins to tickle my scalp.

"I don't want to be here." Her voice has a tremor. I can't tell if she's nervous or about to cry. "I don't know this man and he doesn't owe me anything."

"Don't you want to at least get a look at him?"

"I came here because I thought he might help me. But I can't ask some guy I don't even know for money. I don't even have the right to ask him for advice."

"Then don't. Let's go."

"I'm in this by myself, I see that now." She sounds weary and sad. Now I understand why she came home. She craves unqualified encouragement. She needs to know we love her and we won't judge. So far, Mom and I aren't being what she needs us to be. As a sister, I can do better.

"No, you're not," I tell her, "of course you're not. You've got Mom and me. We're both here for you, no matter what you decide to do."

"It doesn't feel that way." She turns the car on and reverses from the parking space. Half a minute later we're back on the highway heading south. I still don't know what she's going to do about the baby.

< 65 >

The Drive-in

There's no turning lane, so when Chloe puts her signal on and brakes, the traffic behind us slams to an irate stop. I watch in my side mirror as the cars pile up. I count seven before an eighteen-wheeler blocks my view. When the honks begin Chloe frowns. When they grow more insistent, she fidgets. When a tiny opening in oncoming traffic appears she hits the gas so hard her little VW jumps and squeals.

Fifty yards into the turn-off, it's like we've crossed into another world. Grasshoppers and dragonflies attack the windows. Weeds scratch the doors and undercarriage. Bumps jar us and grit coats us.

The remains of the ticket booth mark the entrance – a few feet of jagged brick poking up from the ground. Chloe rolls past the booth and comes to a stop at what used to be the gate. She turns the car off and we sit there, listening to the dry whistle of the wind and staring at the ruins of a defunct cultural pastime.

Posts are all that's left of the perimeter fence. Evenly spaced and splintery, they petition the heavens, Stonehenge of the High Plains. On the opposite side of the lot, surrounded by a mountain of tumbleweeds, the gray screen also points upward. Listing to one side, the top quarter of it collapsed and hanging from one stubborn corner, it

< 66 >

represents the era of my mother's childhood. Between us and the screen the hard dirt is carved into even waves that enable every car to park on a slant facing the screen. Bare poles support heavy rusty boxes – the speakers that hook on to the window. I've seen them in movies.

"What's that?" Chloe points to the right of the giant screen. A dog, but like no dog I've ever seen, slinks from behind the weeds. It runs twenty yards, turns in a circle, races in and out of the fence posts, circles again. Its hind-quarters are low; its tail is full and so long it trails the ground.

"A coyote."

"Why's it acting so crazy?"

"It's trying to distract us because it's got babies stashed somewhere." Like Mom, I'm not one to let a chance to preach pass me by. "Mothers care for their young, even if it means putting themselves in harm's way."

I open my door and get out. The hot wind pushes at me. There are a couple of compact cement buildings in the middle of the huge lot – the concession stand and toilets. Heading in that direction, I hear the car door open and close as Chloe follows. I turn and watch her approach. And the laughter just bursts out of me. She's so damn big and awkward and she's flitting through the weeds as though she's as delicate and graceful as a ballerina. It's been a long time since I really, really laughed, and it feels good.

"What's so funny?"

"You could just send him an email," I tell her. "Or hey, friend him."

We tromp forth. The buildings are in pretty good shape; the doors are intact and locked, the windows filthy but unbroken. The roofs are jagged. After all these years the contained odors still whip through the air – buttered

< 67 >

popcorn and urine. Between the two buildings is a playground – a see-saw with no board, a swing frame with no swing, a merry-go-round that's grounded on one side.

I have no desire to examine a public toilet that's been closed up for fifty years, but I would like to gain access to the concession building. We circle it, looking for an entry point. I make goggles of my hands and try to peer through the window, but the glass is layered with dirt and it's dark in there. I do see shapes, though; something's shoved and piled in the middle of the room – maybe tables and chairs, maybe ancient kitchen equipment.

There are front and back doors and I try both. They're locked. Pulling my trusty screwdriver from my pocket, I force the flat end between the door and the jamb of the back door and, twisting the knob, which is old and loose in its dried-out setting, work the screwdriver back and forth.

"An email's not a bad idea." She's relieved to have been offered a passive solution. "I could just put it out there and leave it up to him."

The knob comes off in my hand. I bend over, peer inside, and, locating the mechanism, press it to the side with the screwdriver. And we're in.

The outside light doesn't reach the deepest shadows of the room so it takes a few minutes to get the layout. Four chairs are turned upside down on each of six tables, and they're pushed against the counter. It's old diner-style furniture, but ugly and dented with ripped upholstery – not worth the trouble it'd be to get it out of here. On the other hand, the gumball machine in the corner is a work of art.

At this point I've got to think about what I will and will not share with my sister – and why. The other night she noticed me carrying the grate and she didn't say anything. I think she just assumed I wanted it as a souvenir. But what

< 68 >

was meant to be a hobby is quickly becoming a lucrative enterprise, and while I realize that Chloe's as poor as I am, looting old buildings is my nest on the ground, not hers.

And that's why, when I see the gumball machine in the corner, I pretend to be only mildly impressed. The stand is heavy wrought iron, painted red, and bolted to the floor. The glass orb is in excellent condition – not a scratch; it's about half full of ancient gum. I don't have a penny to put in the slot, but the handle seems to be in good condition. I squat and examine the moorings. I'm going to need a heavy-duty wrench to get this thing loose. And it's going to be heavy – I'll have to drag it.

"This place is too dirty for me." Chloe's standing in the middle of the floor, disdainful of her surroundings. "Nothing worth seeing here."

"Mom's parents loaded her and her sister into a station wagon in their pajamas and packed sandwiches and popcorn and cokes. They brought their pillows and blankets and saw movies like *Swiss Family Robinson* and *The Sound of Music* and *Pollyanna*."

"Sounds cozy."

At this point, an interesting shape beyond the far end of the counter catches my attention. A pinball machine. I give it a scan – wooden legs, colorful display, no visible cracks or dings. This could be a good find. I take a step toward it but my progress is interrupted by a slight rustle coming from the other side of the counter – and the rustle is followed by a sinister *Shukashukashuka*, a sound both of us recognize. Chloe leaps toward the door with a squeal of alarm. I didn't know a woman so heavily pregnant could move so fast. Not even a rattler can disturb my drug-induced calm. I follow her sedately, disgusted by this unexpected problem. I pull the door closed behind me. One rattlesnake or a whole nest

< 69 >

– how the hell am I going to get that stuff out of there now?

When we get home Chloe races to the television to check the local mid-day broadcast. She doesn't sit down, but watches the coverage standing in front of the screen, swaying from one foot to the other like she's rocking a fretful baby. The footage shows several police cars, a couple of fire engines, and an ambulance, all with their signal lights blinking as though they've been called to an emergency. Uniforms mill in the background as a police spokesman explains about the anonymous tip and the body that at this point is believed to be Johnny Kessler.

"What would you do if you were me?" Chloe asks without turning around.

"Honest to God, Chloe, I don't know."

< 70 >

The Past Catches Up

Part of being in a support group is that we're all expected to stand up periodically and give some sort of accounting of ourselves. I've never been good at speaking in public. I find it amazing that people are not only willing, but eager to share intimate details. Also, given that we're all addicts, I don't believe I have anything to say that hasn't already been said. Because I'm reluctant, Jane has suggested that I follow a reasonable schedule of speaking every six weeks or so; and if I'm struggling to find something to say, I should make a list of pertinent talking points.

This Thursday will mark six weeks since I last spoke, so this afternoon at work I sit behind the counter and contemplate what aspect of my progress I feel comfortable presenting to the group. My pen is poised for list-making, but the piece of paper in front of me remains blank.

One of the recovery steps requires making amends for the harmful things done while under the influence. And lately one of the bad things I did has been on my mind.

About a year ago my friend Brenda and I were meeting some people at High Top, a top-floor bar in one of Dallas's downtown high-rises. Before we got in the elevator Brenda stopped at the ATM and withdrew ten crisp one hundred dollar bills. She folded the cash into her wallet and tucked her wallet into her purse. High Top was packed, dark, and

< 71 >

loud, and when Brenda went to the restroom, leaving her purse in my care, I dug out her wallet and took one of the bills.

Brenda was my friend. Who does something like that to a friend? Part of my current therapy focuses on identifying and retargeting the qualities that compelled me toward addiction in the first place. I'm committed to getting my life back, but I have to ask – fundamentally, have I changed at all? It's becoming clear that addicted or not, my heart beats to a larcenous rhythm. Also, does my tendency to take things that don't belong to me have anything to do with being an addict?

And do I really have to look up Brenda and apologize? She probably never noticed that one of the bills was missing, and if she did, she never would have suspected me, her friend. What would be the result of my coming clean? It might be a step in helping me move forward, but she'd be hurt. She'd hate me. If she forgave me, that'd be for me, not for her, so wouldn't confessing help me and hurt her? This making amends seems self-serving. I'll discuss it with Jane.

As I watch the people pass by out in the mall – and it's Saturday, so there are a lot of them – I feel a rush of envy for the ones carrying shopping bags. It seems to me that becoming a new person requires new clothes, which, even if I have an account that's filling up, I can't buy, because Mom would want to know where the money came from. I'm still wearing the clothes I had in Dallas – professional suits that reflect an authority I don't have, sleek skirts that have no place in the pragmatic panhandle, shoes of soft leather that are losing their shape.

I turn my thoughts back to what I'm going to talk about at group, but so far all I've written is "Brenda". Isn't it bizarre how sometimes you're thinking about some outlandish

< 72 >

possibility, and then it happens? Or someone you once knew is on your mind and they suddenly appear? The next time I glance out into the mall, guess who's coming out of Dillard's and progressing toward the central fountain – Brenda.

I have no desire to see her and I don't want her to see me. A part of me wants to crouch behind the counter in some sort of dramatic gesture of avoidance, but that requires too much energy. My inclination these days is to not overreact. So I remain sedately in my seat and watch as she advances across my field of vision.

Brenda. Lives and works in Dallas. Yet here she is, in the mall in Caprock. What are the odds?

Am I sure it's her? Yes, her long legs, heavy hips, and pounding gait are distinctive, even from this distance. And I'd recognize her brown wavy hair anywhere; it flows like a vibrant waterfall to the small of her back. Looking at her, I recall her nasal voice and the way she called everybody "Sugar" because she couldn't be bothered to remember anybody's name. I also remember how, the night I stole her money, she told me that I had no personal style and that I lacked presence. She had no idea she'd said something mean. It never occurred to her that she hurt my feelings; nor did it occur to her that I had feelings to hurt.

In fact, now that I think about it, it seems like the only thing that brought the two of us together was love of our mutual pal, Coca Blanca. A few seconds ago I was counting her as a best buddy, feeling guilty that I'd stolen from her. But upon being presented with the corporeal reality, my sweet nostalgia has morphed into a hard knot of aversion. Why, I didn't like her at all. The only reason I hung out with her was because she shared. And the only reason she shared was so I'd hang out with her.

< 73 >

She's beyond the fountain. I calmly walk to the front of the store and observe the bounce of her hair as she sails away, a boat on choppy waters. I watch until she disappears through the exit at the far end of the mall.

On Monday morning Jane gives her opinion:

"Apologizing and making amends are two different things," she says. Today she's wearing a pale blue sweater set with brown trousers.

"When did you stop caring about clothes?" I ask. We were both into fashion in high school. What we wore and how we looked was our thrilling daily issue. The pressing of her lips and downward shift of her eyes indicate her genuine dislike of the woman I have become. This hurts and surprises. I thought we were getting along; I thought this mutual disdain was a game we were playing before we went back to being the way we were. There was a time when we were completely candid with one another. But now there are things I don't say because she would disapprove, and things I shouldn't say because what was once a part of our friendship is now considered rude. Having a conversation with her is like tiptoeing through old bones.

"Other things took precedence." Her tone is defensive. "A house, husband, kids. Just because you went into fashion professionally doesn't mean it's the live-all and be-all for everybody. Some of us grow out of things."

And I think how she's grown out of things literally as well as figuratively – a mean thought. On the way to this appointment I stopped by the UPS store and shipped the antique hardware to Candace Weyburn in Portland, Oregon. She's sending the cashier's check care of my bank.

"I didn't go into fashion," I tell her. "I went into journalism. Fashion's just the field I ended up in."

"Because it interests you."

< 74 >

I sigh. Yes, it does interest me. It interests me so much that my desire for a new pair of shoes is almost as strong as my desire for a line of white. That's good, right?

"So what you're saying is that apologizing is personal and making amends isn't?"

"It sounds like you were mad at her at the time. Vengeance isn't honorable but it's understandable. You took her money. So give it back. Send it to her anonymously – no confrontation, no dramatic apology. And you've met the requirement."

This sounds reasonable – except for the actual sending of the money. I'll have to think about that one.

"How are you progressing in finding an area of interest?" She's sure persistent about this hobby business.

"I'm thinking about herpetology."

"And that's the study of – ?"

"Snakes."

"Snakes. Dare I ask why?"

"Don't you think it'd be useful? What if you inadvertently stumble across a rattlesnake? Wouldn't you want to know what to do?"

"I guess I'd high-tail it out of there." She says it in a superior drawl, as though hers is the only rational response. When did her imagination die?

The website about snakes mentioned an electronic repellent which appears to be some sort of strong vibration machine. At sixty bucks, it's not prohibitive; nevertheless, I'd rather not spend the money. Surely there's some similar solution that'll cost nothing.

Later that afternoon I'm sitting in front of my laptop at the kitchen table when the doorbell rings. Mom's due home from work any minute and Chloe's gone to the grocery store. Reluctant to step away from my research about snake

< 75 >

infestations (I've just been advised to rid the area of whatever food supply is drawing the snakes) I drag myself to the front door. Peering through the peephole, I know right away who stands on the other side. I thought Chloe and I looked alike and that we looked like Mom; but Chloe shares features with this guy, too – the broad forehead and square shoulders. I open the door.

"Is Chloe home?" He's handsome for a bald man – even features, upright posture, straight white teeth. Beyond him, parked out on the street, is a silver Mercedes. Nice car.

"She emailed you and now you've come." It's a stupid statement, but I need clarity. Why is he here and what am I supposed to do with him?

Mom's CR-V turns into the driveway. Seeing a visitor on the front porch, she comes to an immediate stop rather than continuing on to the garage. She gets out and her long-ago lover turns, sees her, and marches off to confront.

"We had a kid?" he asks, stopping halfway to her car.

"What in the world?" She steps gingerly across the grass, inspecting foot placement; she's learned to expect gross doggy surprises. Blinking, cocking her head like a curious sparrow, she studies him. The beige flowered scrubs and white support shoes, in addition to the exhausted slant of her shoulders, clearly identify her as a nurse coming off duty.

"You had my baby and you never told me?"

"Henry?" she asks. "Henry Kearney?"

"You were pregnant. I have a daughter."

"Well, I suppose."

"You named her after my dog."

"I liked the name." And then they just stand there staring at each other.

"Mom, are you going to ask him in?" This is rare

< 76 >

entertainment and I want to move things along because I have to get ready for work.

"Do you want to come in?" Mom asks him.

"You haven't changed a bit," he says. Derogatory or complimentary, I can't tell.

I try to study her objectively. Her hair has lost some of its youthful sheen and her face carries a few more wrinkles, but other than that, yes, she looks pretty much the same as she did twenty years ago.

"Come on in," she repeats, taking a step toward the door.

The two move toward where I'm standing and I slide back, making room for them to enter.

"Don't you have to get ready for work?" she asks me.

"I'm Chloe's older sister, Olivia," I tell him, determined to be as obnoxious as possible. "I'm a cocaine addict just out of rehab and Mom is my legal custodian. Chloe's pregnant and just going into her senior year at UT. She's currently undecided about whether to keep the baby or give it to strangers who live in a good school system. It was my suggestion that she email you. And now you're all caught up."

"Olivia, I swear. Go away."

Because I always do what she tells me, except when I don't, I go upstairs to get ready for work.

< 77 >

Food Court Interrogation

Later, at work, I fill Zachary in on this latest development.

"She named Chloe after the guy's dog," I say. "Who'd she name me after?"

His concentration on the sketch in front of him is exaggerated. He's trying to think of a way to evade.

"Tell me."

He's consumed by curiosity about what's going on between Mom and the dermatologist. He's called her several times but it's going to voicemail.

"Come on, tell me."

"It's not a big deal," he says. "She just wanted each of you girls to retain something from your biological fathers."

"Did she name me after his dog? His cat? His hamster?"

"His car."

"Only idiots name their cars."

He shrugs.

"Have you ever had a run-in with a snake?" I slide behind him and look over his shoulder to see what he's working on. Expecting to see a ring setting, I'm surprised to find a pendant design instead. "Gorgeous," I tell him.

"A literal snake or a figurative snake?"

"Literal. A rattler." I shift to his side and lean on the counter, something I know he hates.

"Once when I was a kid."

< 78 >

"What'd you do?"

"Run."

Lately I've been wondering about his life. It's generally understood that he's gay, but don't gay men like to spend time with other gays? He's on our back porch pretty much every night during the summer, and on our couch in front of our fireplace in the winter. His friendship with my mother is solid and comfortable. Considering how much he enjoys drama, his life holds little risk.

"Why aren't you in a relationship?" I ask, knowing it'll irritate him. For someone who's all over everybody else's business, he's fanatically reticent about his own.

"Too much trouble."

"You're quite a catch. Talented, well-off, pretty close to being mentally stable."

"There's nothing as pathetic as an old queen sniffing after a boy toy."

Oh. I understand pride. I was stripped of mine a while back and I'm working hard to regain it.

The phone rings. With a step and hop to reach it, I answer, "Palin's Jewelry."

"Olivia?" It's Chloe.

"Hey, Chloe. Did you meet your father? Is he still there? Mom's not answering her phone."

"Pay quick attention." She speaks in a furtive whisper. "The police were just here looking for you. They're on to you about Johnny Kessler. I overheard the guy tell Mom about a partial print on a plank."

I remain silent, sluggishly processing her spurt of news.

"Mom told them you were home in bed every night last week," she tells me. "Then she told them where you work and I think they're coming to talk to you."

Out in the mall there's a shift in ambience. A sudden

< 79 >

hush followed by an anxious murmur signals that something unexpected is going on. Scanning the central open
area, I see a small posse heading our way – a man in his
fifties flanked by two Caprock PD uniforms. The central
man – medium height, thick torso over thin legs, grim features – wears a worn gray suit, white shirt, no tie. One of
the officers is a stout man with a shaved head; the other is
a petite orange-haired woman who probably doesn't weigh
as much as the gear she carries. With an abrupt "thanks" to
Chloe, I replace the phone in its cradle.

"Heads up," I say. There's no clear reason for the phrase
and Zachary looks up, confused.

I recognize the male officer as soon as he's over the
threshold. Wally Roach. He was a fat-faced bully in middle
school, and his mean little eyes don't indicate a change.

The older man steps forward, presenting a faded badge
in a worn leather holder.

"I'm Detective Rhimes," he says. "We need a few minutes
of your time."

"I can't think of a single reason why." I look flummoxed,
which is an expression I excel in. I've had to deal with cops
a time or two in reference to my substance abuse, and my
proven strategy is to talk without saying anything.

"Just a few questions. An informal conversation at the
food court, that's all."

"Now, wait a minute." This from Zachary, who abhors
the idea of the entire mall witnessing his employee doing a
perp walk to the food court.

"Sir, I could take her downtown, but I'm making this
easy." He looks at me again, quirking a brow in questioning invitation.

"Sure," I say. I come from behind the counter. He
gives a little nod, almost a bow, and opens an arm to give

< 80 >

direction. Catching the combined odors of day-old after-shave and garlic, I pass him and exit the store. The three of them follow me all the way to the food court. It would be a silent entourage, except the gear hanging from the two uniforms creaks, squeaks, bumps, and rattles. The officers are an unintended percussion section. I choose a central table. The area is quiet, with only a few of the tables on the far end occupied.

"You want a coke?" Rhimes asks.

"Sure."

He gives the redhead a look and she moves off to fetch me a soft drink. Wally stands by the table, facing away, hands clasped behind him, chest puffed out. I take a second to assess all the equipment hooked on his belt – phone, gun, cuffs, flashlight, keys. Towering like that, he draws attention.

"So what's this about?" I ask, adding, "I'm doing well with my rehab and I'm following all the rules. My mother watches me like a sentry on steroids." I meet his eyes so he can see that mine are clear. I stretch my hands on the table so he can see that they're steady.

"Someone broke into the Ramey Building. We've got a print that matches yours, and someone saw a car in the area that's similar to yours."

"This has to do with whoever found that kid?"

"Were you in that building?"

"No. Why would I be?"

"How do you explain the print?"

I review my time in the building. The first time I wiped the few places we'd touched, the second time I was doubly careful. I have faith in my system. Also, the way tricky cops do, he's trying to make me think he has more than he has. Chloe said partial on a plank, and those planks were splintery. He's acting like he's got something viable.

< 81 >

"Tell me about this print," I say. "Was it actually inside the building?"

"Our thinking is that someone went in there after dark. If someone was hanging around during the day, there'd be more witnesses." And now he's yammering about nothing, which tells me that's exactly what he has – nothing.

"I'm always where I'm supposed to be," I tell him. "If my mom isn't watching me, my boss is."

"Your mother has to sleep sometime."

"And so do I. Also, my car's a popular model. They're all over town."

The girl cop returns with a drink and sets it in front of me. I frown at Detective Rhimes.

"I don't know why you're here." I move the straw up and down, making a noise, but not drinking. "Shouldn't the concern be what happened to Johnny Kessler instead of who found him?"

"Just dotting the i's and crossing the t's. If you were the one who called in, if you were in that building, it's best if you tell me." Best for him, maybe.

"I have a record for cocaine abuse in Dallas," I tell him as I stand. "I'm here, in my hometown, getting clean. This is harassment. Don't come at me again for no reason."

I walk away. In this situation the drugs are helping instead of hindering – I'm unruffled when ordinarily I'd be trembling all over. But my exit's not clean. Rhimes follows me.

"Just hold on a minute." Quicker than he looks, he shifts in front of me, blocking my way.

"What else could you possibly have to say to me?"

"You're sticking with the program. I can respect that. But, just so you know, we're watching you." His tone is benign but he means it as a threat. I don't take it seriously.

< 82 >

In a day or two he'll have to turn his focus elsewhere. It's the nature of his job. He stands aside and I return to the store to find Zachary waiting.

"What the hell, Olivia?" he asks, rightfully peeved.

"I'm sorry, Zachary. They were questioning me about that body."

"What? Why?"

"I'm a permanent suspect. It goes with the territory."

Because he's known me all my life, he still thinks of me as an earnest little girl. He hasn't quite grasped that I have a criminal record, or what that means.

A few minutes later Wally Roach and his partner come in.

"Olivia Henderson," he drawls. "You remember me?"

"Hello, Wally."

"So I understand you got yourself in some trouble a while back." It gives him pleasure to say so.

His partner stands behind him. I look at her, our eyes meet, and she looks away. I estimate that she's about Chloe's age.

"What can I do for you, Wally?"

"I'm just here following orders. Keeping an eye on a suspect."

"Now, wait a minute – " This from Zachary, indignant that they've come back.

"Sir, we've got a job to do." He dismisses Zachary with a contemptuous glance. It doesn't matter how wealthy or brilliant Zachary is, all Cockroach Wally sees is an old fag. That's just the kind of asshole he is.

"Then do it from a distance," Zachary says. He pinches his lips together in an effort to keep his sarcasm from bursting out. He can be scathing, but now is not the time.

"Trespassing is a crime," Wally tells me. "I don't know

< 83 >

what-all goes on in those other places you been, but here in Caprock we take crime seriously. We're watching you." As he says this last, he does the hokey thing where he points his two fingers at his tiny eyes, then at me. Then he pivots and saunters away. His partner rolls her eyes in weak apology, turns, and trails him out into the mall.

"'Here in Caprock we take crime seriously,'" Zachary mocks.

"Not too seriously if they've got Cockroach Wally on the case. Maybe his eyes look so small because his face is so big."

"They think you're the one who found Johnny Kessler?" he asks. I cringe at the question, only slightly, but he catches it and his eyes light up. "It was you."

"No, it wasn't."

"Cops came here, into my store, for a reason. You're the one. What I don't know is why you were there in the first place."

"It wasn't me."

"Oh please. There's a difference between withholding and outright lying."

"Okay. I'll admit to being there if you agree to let it drop."

"I'll let it drop if you tell me why."

"That's not letting it drop."

"You were in the Ramey Building and you're the anonymous caller."

"No, no, no." I jab my finger toward him and give a serious glare so he'll know I mean it. "You're wrong on that one. I can say with complete honesty that I did not make that call."

He knows me well enough to know when I'm telling the truth. He believes me. Squinting and pressing his lips

< 84 >

together, he gives the matter serious thought. He's imagining it all – the darkness, the dusty interior of the cells, the tight beam of a flashlight illuminating the shadowy contours of a grinning skeleton. And now it's my turn to read his features; his jaw drops and his eyes widen. He's realizing that if I didn't call in the body somebody else did; he's wondering who was with me. I have no friends; I've been isolated and unapproachable since I moved back home. And then it occurs to him.

"No!" His screech is comical. "What were you thinking?"

"She wanted to come. She wouldn't take no for an answer."

"You girls will be in so much trouble if your mother finds out."

"Which'll never happen unless you tell her."

"You're going to owe me. And don't think for a minute that I won't collect."

< 85 >

Bovine Judgment

Around seven-thirty Zachary leaves me in charge of the store and rushes off to grill Mom about what he sardonically refers to as "The Ascension of the Patriarch."

Left to my thoughts, I examine the outcome of our harmless excursion into the Ramey Building. Unintentionally, I've put myself on the cops' radar. Now, like I told Zachary, I'm a permanent suspect. It's a grim reality. On the other hand, I got the fixtures. They were there for the taking, and I made money. Does that make me a thief or an opportunist? Frankly, I don't care. And concerning the interview with Rhimes, I'm disdainful. The only reason he's concentrating on the anonymous caller is because he's unable to figure out what happened to Johnny Kessler.

When I get home Mom and Zachary are out back.

"Where's Chloe?" I ask. "The girl, not the dog." I dump my sweater and purse on the table and flop into my usual chair.

"She's gone to bed."

"What happened? What was it like, seeing him after all these years?" Sliding a cigarette from the pack in the side pocket of my purse, I light it, inhale, tilt my face toward the sky, and release.

"I've just gone through the whole thing with Zachary."

< 86 >

Predictably, she waves her hand around in an effort to clear the smoke.

"So? Go through it again."

"Okay, long story, short. He's really mad at me." Her tone is one of confusion. "He says he feels used and that I set out to deceive him. And he says he wants to be part of Chloe's life."

"What did Chloe think of him?"

"She went to bed before we had a chance to talk."

At the mention of bed, a wave of exhaustion hits me. I say goodnight and head upstairs. I stop at Chloe's door. Her light's out. I give a brief knock and poke my head in. The lump she makes under the covers is barely visible in the darkness.

"Chloe?"

"I'm sleeping."

"Are you alright?"

"I need sleep."

"Thanks for calling earlier, with the warning."

"Goodnight, Olivia."

I close the door and go to my own room, where I fall into bed without changing or washing my face. I sleep better than I've slept in months.

Once a week I meet Sue, my sponsor from the addiction group, at the Starbucks on Belton Avenue. Though we have very little in common and she's twice my age, I like her. She doesn't judge, though sometimes she gets a little preachy; also, she tends to focus on what's going on in her personal sphere, which means very little input is required of me. As usual, Starbucks is bustling. The steamy odor of coffee is pervasive. We've grabbed the last vacant table.

"Did you ever smoke?" I'm longing for a cigarette. Generally when I drink coffee I smoke, which of course isn't

< 87 >

allowed in here, but if I can't indulge I can at least talk about indulging. Also, with a good night's sleep behind me, I should feel energetic and alert; but instead I feel groggy and remote, as though everything around me is taking place several feet away. This effect is enhanced by the caffeine.

"Oh yes, we all smoked," she says. "But we didn't know it was bad for us. What I don't understand is how, in this enlightened age, you could take it up in the first place."

"You're not that old. You smoked in what – the seventies? People knew it was harmful by then."

"But we didn't believe it. When people are young they don't think anything can hurt them."

"And there's your answer." Then I tell her what I tell Mom. "One vice at a time."

"So, how're you doing? Are you going to stand up on Thursday night?"

I tell her I'm thinking about speaking about how I owe money but don't want to pay because I don't like the person I owe it to.

"Hm. Not a very inspirational story to share with the group."

"No." For several seconds we sit in silence and contemplate the impetus it takes to transition from thinking to acting. Though I like Sue, I have other things to do, so I grow antsy as she talks about her granddaughters, her Mahjong friends, and her neighbor's elderly cats. Usually we linger over our coffee, but today I tell her I have to get to work. And I've told Mom that after my meeting with Sue I've got an appointment with Jane. I've finagled myself an extra couple of hours.

I get to the Meskar place around ten o'clock and park in the same place as before. Because I scratched my back last time, today I grabbed an old wool blanket from the

< 88 >

garage; it'll provide protection from the barbed wire. I toss the blanket over the fence so it'll be waiting for me when I get back.

It's a lovely morning. Clouds stretch across the blue sky like pulled cotton, the air is cool and fresh, and the slant of the sun on the mesquite creates intriguing shadows. In an hour the wind will have picked up and the sun will be fierce.

Last time I had the area to myself as I hiked across the country. Today, several hundred yards to the south, but on the same side of the fence, several cows lift their heads and look toward me. As soon as I drop from the top of my car to the other side of the fence they begin to drift in my direction.

In my muddled state, the mild exercise doesn't feel good. My breathing is labored and I begin to sweat even though my pace is sluggish, my exertion minimal. I've been forbidden heavy exercise, but I'm thinking some light yoga would do me good. Something to discuss with the cardiologist at my next appointment.

By the time I reach the house, I'm in the middle of the herd. The cattle kick up dust and they smell awful. They snort and some of them have nasty slime hanging from their snouts.

When I haul the ladder to beneath the balcony, they mill around the bottom and offer encouraging moos. My new friends.

I brought my backpack empty and I walk through the house and fill it up with as much as I can carry. Smaller lamps, a matching pair of large Waterford vases, a scalloped Delft serving dish. I empty out the silverware drawer, taking the entire set of sterling flatware which I'm pretty sure is quite old and quite valuable.

By now the backpack is heavy. I exit through the front

< 89 >

door only to find a couple of cows waiting, watching from the other side of the porch railing.

"Don't judge me," I tell them as I circle the house and put the ladder away.

The herd escorts me back to my car. I feed the backpack full of breakables through the barbed wire, set it down carefully and, covering my back with the folded blanket, crawl under. The thick wool provides a fine shield.

I haven't gone a mile toward town when my dethroned master calls.

Come to me, come to me, my faithful, my dearest, my friend.

Oh, cocaine, cocaine, my heart, my brain. A hole in my soul gapes and sucks me in. The me I'm struggling to become disappears into a pit filled with yearning and desperation.

Pulling to the shoulder, I stop the car, close my eyes, and prepare to ride it out. I want, I want, I want something that I can't, I can't, I can't have. I combat it by defining it. It's only neurons firing in my brain. Xanax will suppress it.

For five minutes I keep my eyes tightly closed and concentrate on breathing slowly, deeply. By the time the yearning becomes manageable, I've been clutching the steering wheel so long and so hard that the muscles of my hands are cramped. The inside of my head is throbbing as I mourn the loss of who I used to be. Then I acknowledge who I am now – a fool, a person without control, a loser scorned by idiots like Wally Roach. I'm sure I'm supposed to put some kind of positive spin on this, but who can find a flicker of optimism in this dismal truth?

I can. I must. Otherwise I'll never get better. I remind myself that the bouts with temptation are growing less intense and further apart. I survived this one and I'll survive the next one. Soon they'll be gone completely.

< 90 >

Hello Allison

When I get home I leave my car parked in the driveway because I've got time to wash it before getting ready for work. I pass Chloe's closed door on the way to my room, where I stash the Meskar items under the bed. Exchanging my heavy boots for flip-flops, I return outside where I grab a sponge and fill a bucket with soapy water.

In the trunk are a few items that comprise my snake-repelling kit. Here's what I've gathered so far:

A twenty-year-old boom box, because snakes don't like vibrations and the busted boom box I found in the garage emits a sibilant pulsation that follows the bass line in the most annoying way.

Next to the boom box is an industrial sprayer and kerosene, which leads to another interesting fact – snakes also don't like kerosene. I imagine a snake cringing in horror as I give it a good dousing. The sprayer and kerosene cost less than fifteen dollars at Wal-Mart, a reasonable investment if the gumball machine is worth what I hope it is. The seminal factor seems to be the manufacture date – before 1940, worth four hundred; after 1940, a hundred and fifty. The pinball machine could bring in as much as seven hundred, but it'll be heavy and storing it will be a problem. Maybe I should post a picture of it and see if I get a buyer before going to the trouble of removing it.

< 91 >

The trunk also holds a long stick with a mechanical grip on the end. Also from Wal-Mart, the pharmacy department, twelve dollars. It's intended for stroke victims or people who are too stiff to bend or reach. Its purpose in my situation is obvious, though I hope not to be forced into physical combat with a rattler over a bubble gum machine.

And I've got a pair of knee-high leather boots to protect my lower legs just in case the snake(s) gets too close. I grabbed these out of the dustiest darkest corner of Mom's closet. As far as style, I cannot envision more unattractive footwear – flat black, stacked two-inch heels, toes rounded like hard little bowls, and overkill on the closures – a zipper up the back, shoestrings up the front, and a buckled strap at the ankle.

I'm massaging soapy water into the hood, a task that never fails to soothe, when Chloe steps through the gate.

"I'm in labor," she says.

"It's too early. Anyway, Mom's at work and I need to get ready – "

She emits a primal screech, a horrendous sound that scratches my eardrums. Collapsing against the fence, she wraps her thin arms beneath her massive belly as though she can hold the baby in. Her whole abdomen shifts and rolls beneath the straining T-shirt, which freaks me out. The contraction lasts about twenty seconds and when she comes out of it her face has turned splotchy brown and her eyes are bulging and flooded with tears.

"It's too soon," I say again, but weaker this time.

"I've got a bag packed. In my closet."

"But Chloe, it can't be time. Mom's not here."

She waddles to the other side of my wet car, opens the passenger door, gets in, and just sits there staring forward. I stand unmoving, soapy sponge dripping from my hand.

< 92 >

What the hell? It takes several seconds for my brain to catch up to the situation. Then I drop the sponge in the bucket, quickly rinse the soap off my hood, and go inside and fetch her overnight bag.

"Your water better not break while you're sitting in my car," I tell her as I slide behind the wheel. I hand her my phone, saying, "You've got some calls to make."

On the way to the hospital she calls Mom's floor and leaves a message that she's on her way in. And she calls Zachary and tells him I won't be coming in and why. And she calls the father she met for the first time yesterday. The call she neglects to make is to the adopting parents.

Apparently, at Mom's instigation, Chloe pre-registered, so check-in is no more than signing her name and stepping into a wheelchair. I follow along as she's rolled down the hall, into an elevator, down another hallway, and to the birthing room. We're there for no more than three minutes when Mom enters. She aims one of her speaking looks at me – she wants to know if Chloe has made a decision. I shrug.

Signs are monitored and announced – four minutes apart, eight centimeters dilated, everything just as it should be. Mom and I are given cotton cover-ups and surgical masks. We slip into them, leaving the masks to hang at our throats until they're needed. Medical personnel whisk in and out as my little sister lies on a thin hard mattress, head elevated, knees up and spread. Mom hovers on one side of the bed and I hover on the other, both of us encouraging, panting right through the contractions with her, though Chloe doesn't appreciate our efforts; she seems to have developed some sort of hypersensitivity.

"Stop breathing on me," she says, then, "Don't touch me." Then, "The light's hurting my eyes." A few seconds

< 93 >

later, "All this noise is driving me crazy." This is under-standable; pings and dongs and beeps seem to be coming at us from all sides. And finally, "This place smells like a hospital."

"Duh," I say, growing impatient.

We fall into a cycle. Chloe tenses through a contraction, catches her breath, finds something else to complain about, has another contraction – and we offer supportive phrases like "You can do it." and "Stick with it." and "You're doing great." This lasts a couple of hours – at which time, Mom reaches a point where she can no longer remain silent about Chloe's plans.

"What names have you picked out?" she asks in the most neutral tone she can muster.

"I haven't picked out any names."

"No matter what you decide, surely you have the right to name your own child." Not quite so passive this time.

My little sister snarls at Mom like a jungle animal – and she looks like one, too. Her hair, which started out clean, is matted and dull. Her face has become a brown mask. Deep trenches stretch from the edges of her nostrils to the sides of her lips. I can see clearly what she will look like when she's sixty.

That's when Chloe's father slips into the room. Dressed neatly in khakis, a tucked-in golf shirt, and loafers, he brings an air of calm to this exhausted room.

"They told me I can only stay for a minute – only a couple of people allowed."

"Henry," Mom says. "What are you doing here?"

He sends her a nasty glare and, without responding, moves further into the room. When he looks at Chloe his expression softens and a broad smile lights his face.

"Hey there, kiddo," he says. "How're you doing?"

< 94 >

I don't understand this guy. He only found out yesterday that he had a kid. And that his kid is having a kid. Why is he here? Wouldn't a normal person run far away as fast as possible?

"I want you to stay," Chloe tells him.

"He can't." Mom is clearly disturbed.

"I want him to." Chloe appeals to the nurse who's in charge of the delivery room. "Can they wait outside? He's the one I want with me."

"Oh good God!" Mom says, grabbing my arm and pulling me with her across the room and through the swinging door.

"Did what I think just happened really happen?" I ask. "Were we just expelled from the delivery room?"

Clearly confounded, Mom heads toward the chairs that line the other side of the wide corridor. She collapses into one of them and, bending forward, holds her head in her hands. I take the seat next to her.

"I pushed too hard," she says. "Why do I always push too hard?" Her sad words are aimed at the floor. "I couldn't let it go for even a little while and now she's chosen some stranger over me."

At that moment Zachary turns the corner at the end of the hallway. As soon as he sees Mom's defeated posture his eyes twinkle – but he quickly replaces the merriment with long-faced sympathy. His reaction delights me. What are we here for if not to provide drama for Zachary?

"Don't you have wedding rings to design in Barbados?" I ask.

"Costa Rica, leaving day after tomorrow." He spreads a comforting palm across Mom's bowed shoulder. "How's Chloe? What's wrong? What's going on?"

"She kicked us out of the delivery room," I tell him.

< 95 >

"No." Mom straightens. "No, it's me she kicked out, not you. You need to go back in there."

"She wanted us both gone."

"It's really just me she's mad at. Please, Olivia. One of us needs to be with her."

Chloe's miserable groan reaches us. Mom's probably right; she usually is. I turn and go back in, taking a big breath before entering, as though I'm going under water. I approach the bedside quietly, hoping like a fool that maybe Chloe won't notice. When her wild eyes register my arrival I expect her to protest, but she doesn't.

"Just do what comes naturally from here on in," the midwife tells Chloe. To me, she says, "Mask on."

I comply. Chloe's dad already has his mouth and nose covered. Looking down, I can actually see the baby moving as it's being pushed through the birth canal. I feel bad for Chloe – that's got to hurt. And, as happens so often lately, I take a few seconds away from the scene that's playing out right in front of my eyes, to contemplate how I'm not really present in the life I'm living. It's the drugs. Insomnia, exhaustion, detachment. Glancing up, I meet Chloe's dad's eyes.

"A new life," he says. "A miracle. Happening right here in front of us."

"Do I call you Henry?" I ask.

"And I'll call you Olivia. We'll be friends." I decide he's goofy, perhaps even naïve, but innocuous.

We return our attention to Chloe's shifting stomach. Half an hour later Chloe's daughter is born.

"Allison." Having named her child, she closes her eyes and relaxes into the pillow. Tears seep out, making a trail. She's too weary to do anything other than lie there.

"Allison," Henry repeats. "Beautiful. I like it."

< 96 >

When Mom comes in Chloe refuses to speak to her. She's decided to keep her baby and, like a prophet, I can see where this is going. If somebody, somehow, doesn't put a stop to it, Chloe's going to blame Mom every time she's tired, every time the baby cries, every time she has to go without, every time, every time.

On Thursday morning Henry Kearney picks Chloe and her baby up from the hospital. They come to the house, but instead of settling in, Chloe packs two suitcases and Henry carries them to the car. This only takes about half an hour, during which time I sit on the couch and cuddle my sleeping niece.

"You're the most wonderful, sweetest, cutest baby I've ever seen," I tell her, though admittedly I've never been exposed to that many tiny humans. A couple of Chloe's features are obvious – the sloping of the nose, the pale curling lashes.

"I'll be back to get my car in a few days," Chloe tells me after she completes a final sweep of the downstairs.

"Please don't do this," I say. "You're an adult and you made an adult decision. It's not right to punish Mom for it."

"She pressured me. She made me feel like a monster – and now my baby isn't going to have the life she could have had."

And then she closes the door.

< 97 >

Peppering the Grass

After Chloe's gone I'm left sitting on the couch completely at a loss. How am I going to tell Mom? How is she going to react? And Zachary's in Costa Rica, which means he's not here to help me break it to her.

So I sprawl on the couch, my arms still warm from holding the baby, and let my mind drift for a few minutes. I've got to speak at group tonight and I still haven't come up with anything to say. I'm weighing the money I owe Brenda against the money I owe Geraldine, the friend who helped me out with my major payments last year. I owe Geraldine a lot more than I owe Brenda, so it wouldn't be as painful to pay Brenda, but I like Geraldine more. Frankly, the thought of letting go of any amount makes it so I can't breathe. I should get up and get ready to go to work, but I'm having difficulty finding motivation. Also, I plan to leave a little early because I need to stop by the bank and sign the deposit slip for the check I got for the hardware in the Ramey Building.

Bored with my pointless mental meandering, I turn on the local news to see Detective Rhimes giving an interview about the findings concerning Johnny Kessler's death. He was stabbed. There are no clues to follow, no hints as to what he was doing in the abandoned building, no closure other than the reality of his body.

< 98 >

In a brief interview, Detective Rhimes insists that the department has done all it can do. They examined the area around the body and found no evidence to follow. They interviewed his friends from high school – which they also did when he went missing – and learned nothing other than that, as far as anybody knew, he had no reason to be in the Ramey Building, and he was not involved in any sort of miscreant behavior. The autopsy revealed three wounds to his mid-section, the fatal one to his heart.

"Sometimes we just don't know." Rhimes's sorrowful drawl effectively closes the discussion, leaving the interviewer and the viewers perplexed.

How can this be? Caprock is a small city with a low crime rate. People here are honest. They work hard and look after their families. Parents trust that when their son goes to his part-time job, he'll come home. "Sometimes we just don't know." Is this the only answer the Kessler family is going to get? It's odd how this has nothing to do with me, but it has everything to do with me. I feel suspended and bereft. Somehow I'm part of a violent act perpetrated upon someone I never knew.

My phone rings and I dig it out of my pocket. It's Mom.

"You don't have to worry about telling me," she says. "I already heard. One of the nurses from obstetrics told me."

"She just needs a few days."

"I need you to do me a favor," she tells me. "There are a couple of boxes of ground pepper in a bag on the kitchen counter. Would you go out and sprinkle them over the front lawn?"

"What?"

"I hear it repels dogs." Oh dear. This topic isn't going away.

"Okay," I say, clearly dubious.

< 99 >

Five minutes later I'm peppering the grass. It's a hot day and the grass is crunchy beneath my sandals. Mom's right. I don't usually venture into the front yard – we tend to hang out in the back – but there are at least fifteen piles of dog shit out here, maybe twenty. And they're from a big animal, too. I step carefully around them pointing the rectangular container of store-brand ground pepper at the grass and squeezing, trying for even distribution. Beth Ann, the quilter across the street, steps out of her front door, shades her eyes, and watches me for a minute to see what I'm doing. When she figures it out she shakes her head and returns inside.

A woman and her German shepherd walk by on the sidewalk. I recognize them; they pass this way once or twice a week. The dog's hind quarters drag and hang low and he shuffles carefully, like he's in pain. Twice, between one driveway and the next, one of his hips gives out, causing him to lean and stagger. Seeing what I'm doing, the woman smirks, doesn't greet me, just continues tugging her dog along. I eye the white plastic bag she's got tied to the handle of the leash. It's got something brown in it – and I wonder, isn't that the same plastic bag I saw her carrying last time I saw her walk by? I knew a woman in Dallas who didn't like to pick up after her dog, so she carried a bit of brown felt in a grocery bag so people would think she picked up. Is that what's going on here? And, oh great. Mom's obsession is contagious. She's got me suspecting the poop bags of people I don't even know.

I stop by the bank on the way to work, depositing twenty-four hundred and eighty dollars. The thought of the money causes a tightening in my chest; my sluggish heart wants to dance, but can't quite manage to overcome the restriction put on it by the Propranolol. Inside my head I'm shouting

< 100 >

– Look! I have almost three thousand dollars! It's mine! And someday my secret money will help me start a new life in a town where people listen to radio stations other than religious ones. And a woman isn't forced to buy her clothes at Sears or Dillard's because there are classy boutiques whose sole aim is to offer unique styles to the individual, rather than factory-sewn synthetics for the masses.

Because Zachary's out of town, I work a long shift – noon to closing. Karen's on from opening to four and she spends at least half of our overlapping hours on the phone with her daughters. Apparently they're packing for some kind of church youth retreat and they're throwing tantrums because electronic devices are forbidden.

"It's so unfair," Karen says. "Their Bibles are on their Kindles and now I have to go out and buy two Bibles. One Bible is expensive enough. But I always have to buy two of everything. Nobody ever gets that twins cost twice as much."

More of the same for the whole five remaining hours of her shift. I'm so relieved when she walks out the door that I get weepy from the fatigue that comes from remaining politely receptive when what I long to do is reach into her mouth and yank out her tongue.

When I get off work there's a cop car parked behind my car. The silhouette of a large head tells me that Wally Roach is keeping an eye on me, just like he said he would. Presumably the small outline riding shotgun is his mute partner. He follows me as I pull out of the parking lot and on to the highway, and he's still with me when I get off the highway and turn into St. John's. I give his car a friendly wave as I enter the building.

I'm late to group but everybody understands. We all work and a retail job comes with retail closing hours. It

< 101 >

seems Sue has put it around that I'm going to give my tes-
timony, so I'm encouraged to take the podium the second
I enter the room. In short, everybody's been waiting on me
and they're ready to go home.

I planned to talk about step four, but when it comes to
it, I haven't acted on the step and – well, I'll just admit it
– I have no intention of doing so in the near future. While
I believe in the program, the money in that account is too
precious for me to touch for any reason. It represents inde-
pendence. It represents my future.

So, poorly delivered, broken by awkward pauses and too
much fidgeting, here's what I manage to say without really
saying anything:

"I'm grateful to my sponsor, Sue, for putting up with
me. She's a good listener and she's wise, too. And I'm grateful to all of you for your help and inspiration. Every day
gets a little easier, though sometimes it's hard to stay on
track. I'm grateful to my mother's good friend who gave me
a job when no one else would. And I'm grateful that my
sister had a baby girl a couple of days ago and that both my
sister and her baby are healthy."

The last brings an enthusiastic clap and I step away
from the podium. Jane would be disappointed. I know Sue
is – her lips are pressed together and she gives me a cold
appraising glare as I approach her to say good-bye. One by
one, the other members straggle toward the door.

"Not exactly burdened with substance," she says, tucking
her knitting into her bag.

"I'm sorry." There's no reason to deny it. "I just didn't
have anything of substance to say."

"Here." She holds out a little yellow gift bag. I peek
inside to find a tiny pair of pink knitted booties.

Tears fill my eyes and make everything blurry. The

< 102 >

booties are so cute and the baby isn't even around so I can put them on her little feet.

"The baby's name is Allison," I tell her. "She's just beautiful."

"Are you okay?"

"Just tired I guess," I say. Speaking in front of people is difficult for me. This isn't the first time I've fallen apart after something like this. "It hasn't been the best day."

"I'll walk out with you."

Together we stroll to the parking lot. Wally's police car is parked out by the curb.

"It'll be okay, Olivia. You're getting there."

All I can muster is a sigh. I don't like myself very much right now.

"Good night," she says when we separate to go to our cars. "Have a good sleep."

Cockroach Wally follows me home. How long will I be seeing his headlights in my rear view mirror? I guess nothing much happens in Caprock. He must be bored out of his rock-hard little mind.

< 103 >

A Go at the Bubble Gum Machine

As usual I have trouble settling into sleep. I don't attain more than a shallow doze all night, coming fully awake between each nonsensical dream. At around five-thirty I hear Mom stirring downstairs. She'd already gone to bed last night when I got in. Since I'm not sleeping anyway I decide to get up and have a cup of coffee with her before she goes to work.

Steaming cup in hand, hip propped on the broad sill of the big window in the dining room, she peers out at the dark front yard. The only light on downstairs reaches from the distance of her bedroom at the back of the house.

"What's going on?" I ask quietly, moving up next to her to see what she's looking at.

"Watch. He just got here."

A golden lab is shifting through the shadows on the lawn. No master in sight. The dog lifts his leg and pees on the sign.

"Dogs can't read," I tell her.

"I should have gotten the one with the picture instead of words."

Head down, he follows his nose around the grass. It's not long before he releases a sneeze that shakes him from his head to the tip of his tail.

"That's what I'm talking about," Mom says, pleased.

< 104 >

Another sniff, another bone-racking sneeze.

"See, it's working." At least something is going the way she wants it to.

Then he assumes the position and drops a pile right on the corner of the grass where the driveway meets the sidewalk.

"Damn it," she says. Rising, she wanders back to her bedroom.

I go back to my room for my spiritual time. Today is an Old Testament day. I close my eyes, separate the pages, place my finger, and open my eyes. I'm pointing at Ecclesiastes 2:14.

The wise man's eyes are in his head, but the fool walks in darkness. And yet I know that one fate befalls them both.

I like this passage. Straightforward and grim, it suits my current mindset. My interpretation: There are smart people and stupid people and the one thing they have in common is that they all die.

Content with my analysis, I slap the book shut. And immediately chastise myself. The goal is to ponder the meaning, to apply it to my life. So I spend a few minutes with my eyes closed trying to focus on the passage. I even say a brief prayer inside my head – *God, show me the meaning.* But nothing new comes. It says what it says. We all die.

As soon as Mom leaves for work I head out.

Having been followed by Wally Roach last night, I check my mirrors to make sure he hasn't taken it into his head to watch me every minute of every day – but no, apparently he only intends to keep tabs during his shift.

I bump into the weedy lot of the drive-in at seven-thirty, cultivating the foolish notion that if I'm early enough the snake, or snakes, will still be asleep. Unlike last time when we hiked in, this time I bounce my car all the way to the

< 105 >

building, back it up to the door, and open the trunk. The morning sun streaming through the clouds casts pink over the whole eastern third of the sky. The breeze is cool and carries the combined sweet scents of milkweed and the feedlot five miles to the west.

The first part of my plan is to turn on the boom box and vibrate the hell out of the place, but I'm reluctant because it's so peaceful out here. Pragmatism conquers. No time to be sentimental over the country air. I have to be at work at noon and I have an appointment with Jane before that. That gives me a little over two hours to get this done. I open the door of the building and remain motionless for several seconds as I listen for movement. Nothing.

After returning to the car and exchanging my sandals for Mom's hideous boots, I remove the boom box from the trunk, place it in the doorway, and aim it toward the inside. I turn the volume up as loud as it'll go. All that comes out of the busted speakers is a hissing booming bass line. If the snake was asleep before, it's awake now.

After allowing fifteen minutes for the rattler to clear out, I progress to the next step – the kerosene. I hold the spray bottle in my left hand, point and work the nozzle with my right. Since the snake was behind the counter, I spray in that direction first. And after I get that area good and wet, I turn to the opposite side and spray there until the only part of the room that's dry is a straight path from the doorway to the gumball machine. If that snake wants to get at me he'll have to cross a whole lake of kerosene.

The stand is fixed to the concrete floor by six bolts and I'm expecting them to be difficult – rusted, cemented by grit, and painted over; it'll take strength and tenacity to get them to budge. To that end, tucked into my handy backpack, are a heavy wrench, a screwdriver, and a small can

< 106 >

of WD-40, all lifted from Mom's tool box in the garage. Also, I've brought along a Thermos of extremely hot water, just in case rinsing or a change of surface temperature will loosen things up.

At this point I turn the boom box off. If that snake gets aggressive I want to hear it coming.

I start by saturating all the bolts with WD-40, which has no effect at all because the oil can't penetrate through God-only-knows how many layers of industrial paint. I dig at the joints with the screwdriver, managing to crack the paint. Hot water, wipe it down, WD-40, try again. No give whatsoever. More hot water. I bang on the bolts with the head of the wrench. More WD-40. I dig at the bottom of the stand, hoping the concrete floor will crumble; it doesn't. Forty-five minutes into it, my hand slips while jabbing at a seam with the screwdriver, causing one of my fingernails to bend back and roughing up one of my knuckles; but I also manage to make one of the bolts wiggle. At the end of the two hours I've allowed myself, I've worked two bolts free. Packing up my few items, reluctant to leave the job unfinished, I pull the door closed behind me. I didn't have time to check out the pinball machine, but I'll be back tomorrow.

"You smell like gas," is Jane's greeting.

"Splashed some when I was filling up."

Today she's wearing burgundy pants with a white twin set, which makes her golden hair look dull and the pink tones of her face look too pink.

"Some people can wear white," I tell her, "but you're not one of them. With your coloring you should stick to jewel tones – blues, reds, greens. You'd look good in black, but there'll come a time when it'll make you look old, so watch out for that."

< 107 >

"Thanks for the fashion advice." She crosses her arms over her breasts and her legs at the knees, protecting herself from any further comments I might make about her appearance.

"Hey, I'm a never-ending font."

"I heard Chloe had her baby."

"Did you also hear that she took that baby and moved in with a man she's only known for three days?"

"My understanding is that the man is her father."

"She's just using him."

"What do you mean?"

"He seems like a nice man, but she's staying with him to get back at Mom."

"Does it bother you that Chloe is building a relationship with her father?"

"What, you think I have daddy envy?"

"Have you ever been in a long-term relationship?"

"Sure. I was in a relationship with Mr. Snow and it almost killed me."

"Have you considered that your habit of personalizing your addiction is counterproductive?" At this point she rises, shifts behind her desk, and opens a drawer. After a few seconds of digging around, she waves a small tube of Neosporin and a Band-Aid and brings them to me. I guess I look puzzled because she says, "Your knuckle."

Sure enough, the knuckle I banged earlier is bloody. Several layers of skin are peeled back and it looks hot and sore. I hadn't even noticed it. I accept the ointment and Band-Aid and apply and wrap, which is awkward. She doesn't offer to help.

"I'm not necessarily talking about a romantic relationship," she says, settling back into her seat. "I'm talking about connecting with another person, any person."

My friendship with her back in high school is the longest

< 108 >

friendship I've ever had. People tend to get fed up with me. I arrive late and leave early. I break promises. I borrow and never return. I don't do favors but I expect them. I know these things about myself.

"I spoke last night at group," I tell her.

"Oh – and how'd that go?"

"Sue didn't think I went deep enough. But what can I say? I'm not a deep person."

She leaves my flippant remark hanging there, causing it to take on an unintended significance.

"I've come to the attention of local law enforcement," I finally say.

Her only response is a raised brow.

"Wally Roach," I tell her. "He likes that I've run into some trouble. He's still a bully."

"More creep than bully. He'd started shaving his head last time I saw him."

"Huh. As if his face didn't look fat enough."

"Welcome to your new reality. You're an addict with a record. People like Cockroach Wally are allowed to give you a hard time and you have to figure out how to handle it."

So I guess this is the purpose behind these counseling sessions – giving my therapist the opportunity to make herself feel wise by pointing out what I already know.

< 109 >

Three Tiny Puffs

That afternoon Karen asks me for a favor. She's on the schedule to work until three, but she wants to leave work at one because she has some errands to run before picking up the girls.

"Please, please, Olivia, just punch me out at three." Conspiratorial and presumptuous, her tone rankles. "Zachary will never know. And I need the hours. Twins are expensive."

It's the kind of thing one hourly-wage-earner does for the other, but only if they're friends. And she and I are not that. And how stupid is she that she thinks I would do this sneaky favor for her when Zachary's been a part of my life forever? How can she be so obtuse that she's unaware of where my loyalty lies? Also, I've been and done many things that I'm not proud of, but I've always been an ethical employee. I don't know why; my conscience doesn't usually intrude. And, too, if she takes off early there's no one to cover during my afternoon break. It would never occur to her that I desperately look forward to my daily hot migration to the ugly square of sidewalk where society allows me to smoke. Her self-absorption makes me want to get back at her; it makes me want to hurt her a little bit.

"Sure," I tell her. Then as soon as she disappears into the mall I go to the back and insert her time card – 1:03. Principled and spiteful. I'm complex. By one-fifteen I'm

< 110 >

longing for a cigarette, though ordinarily my break time isn't until two-thirty.

Later in the afternoon the phone rings. The ID is blocked.

"Palin's Jewelry."

"I'm trying to reach Olivia Henderson." The hollow hum in the background tells me he's calling from a call center.

"May I ask what this is in reference to?"

"Is this Olivia Henderson?"

"I know her. I can get her a message."

"I'm calling with Amalgamated Disbursement."

A collection agency. They were calling when I lived in Dallas. I figured they'd track me down eventually. Back then my strategy was to avoid, obfuscate, and, when I had to, outright lie. But I've grown since then; I'm learning to take responsibility.

"This is Olivia," I say. "Just tell me how much I owe and I'll add your name to the list."

"Two thousand eight hundred and ninety-two on your Neiman's card." While it's an odd coincidence that this amount is so close to what I have in my secret account, my first thought is no, no, no, I will not use my new money to pay off an old debt. I bought the clothes two years ago. Classics that were a necessary part of my Dallas wardrobe – three jackets, six shells, three pairs of straight-legged pants, three A-line skirts that fall just below the knee and make me look thin as a stick, and a pair of classic black pumps that could stand to be replaced. I'm wearing the burgundy jacket, ivory shell, and navy skirt right now. I should feel shame for wearing clothes I never paid for, but I don't. What I actually feel is bored resignation. Here it comes – more of the same. More debt, more demanding of payment, more of my single past mistake reverberating with the force of a thousand mistakes.

< 111 >

"I can make payments on it just like I'm doing with everybody else I owe," I tell him. "The most I can afford is twenty-five a month."

"Look, Miss Henderson. You owe the whole sum, not twenty-five a month."

"It's all I can do. Come on – I'm not the first person you've worked with."

"Don't you want to clear your debt?"

"Sure. But I'm broke."

"You should have thought of that when you spent money you didn't have."

"Take it or leave it."

"It's not worth the effort."

I disconnect fully aware that now he knows where to find me, he'll keep calling and demanding the full sum. And I'll have to go back to avoiding, obfuscating, and lying.

The next call is from Zachary.

"How are things?"

"Great. When are you coming home?"

"Tomorrow morning. I'll be in around noon. How's your mom?"

"Obsessing about dog poop."

"To be expected. Remember how I kept quiet about that thing I know and now you owe me?"

"Stand in line. I owe everybody."

"I've decided how you can pay me back."

"Okay." I'm wary. Zachary's creative nature often leads to outlandish ideas.

"Somebody I know has something that belongs to me."

I know the story. We all know the story. He's been going on about it for years. His cousin, Leticia, has possession of all the family documents and pictures, and, for some reason (probably because of something mean Zachary said or did,

< 112 >

but he never owns up to his part) she refuses to turn them over to him or even allow him access. It's all very petty. In this age of printers and high quality photo refurbishment, it's just stupid that she doesn't copy the whole mess off and send it to him. There wouldn't even have to be contact.

"The photos of my great-grandparents," he intones. "My grandfather's immigration papers. My grandmother's journal from when she was a prairie schoolteacher and lived in a dugout. She was like a real Laura Ingalls Wilder – did I ever tell you that?"

"You do know that Laura Ingalls Wilder was real – right? I've never understood why you don't just hire a lawyer. He'd write a letter threatening to sue and she'd turn over the stuff."

"Why should I pay a lawyer to get what's mine in the first place?" he asks, adding, "I know exactly where she keeps all of it. In a box in the closet in her back room." He's the richest person I know and also the cheapest.

"Look, Zachary, I don't understand how, in your mind, exploring an abandoned building translates into breaking and entering."

"Trespassing is trespassing no matter how you dress it up," he says.

"We could get arrested. We could get shot."

"Leticia goes to choir practice every Tuesday night from seven-thirty to ten. She never locks her back door." Do I want to know how he came by this information? No, I don't believe I do. "We'd be in and out in ten minutes. All you'd have to do is go with me just to keep an eye out."

"Hmm. I'll think about it." I tell him to have a good flight and we disconnect. I'm not proud that my first thought is, what's in it for me? Nothing material, that's for sure. But it'd be a chance for me to help Zachary, who can

< 113 >

JEN WALDO

be a pain but has been supportive during this whole hellish ordeal. The upside is that it's reciprocation that won't cost me a thing.

What I do next is out of necessity. I take a few puffs off a cigarette in the back room. Mall security could fine me a couple of hundred dollars if they find out – and so to keep that from happening, I turn on the small desk fan and spray air freshener right into the whirling blades while I'm releasing my noxious but glorious cloud. It kind of works. The ventilation ducts of the whole mall are connected, which causes the odor of floral-scented cigarette smoke to travel to the furthest reaches of the mall – the department store fitting rooms, restrooms, back offices, the arcade, the food court. Everywhere. No one is able to tie the infraction to any specific starting point and for the whole rest of the day everyone in the mall is suspicious of everyone else.

At one point the two mall cops, Carol and Mickey, pay me a visit.

"Only you working today?" Mickey asks, glaring at the closed cabinets behind the counter.

"No. Karen's on her break." If I tell them she's not here they'll know for sure it was me. I'm one of only a handful of mall employees that visit the designated smoking area.

"Someone's been smoking in our mall," he explains.

"I can tell. Probably some customer in one of the bathrooms."

"Mind if we take a look in the back room?"

"Go ahead." There's nothing for them to find. I dropped my ashes in the lid of the can of air freshener and wrapped my extinguished butt in a paper towel and tucked them both into my purse, which I locked in the safe.

They go to the back and sniff as they shift things around on the desk. I hang in the doorway and watch them. After

< 114 >

a few minutes they give up and return to the front of the store.

"Smoking in public places is against the law," Mickey says over his shoulder as the two of them saunter back out into the mall.

All this fuss over three tiny puffs.

< 115 >

Checking on Chloe

I look up Leticia Palin on the city's residential website to get her address. Before leaving the store I call Mom and tell her I'm stopping to buy cigarettes, a lie that buys me a few minutes so I can take a detour by Zachary's cousin's house, which is a block off the freeway at the downtown exit. Some of the older sections of town have been revamped. This isn't one of them. The houses are uniformly run-down. Screens curl, bricks crumble, and roofs sag. The yards are more weed than grass and there are more dead trees than live ones.

It's a cloudless night with a dazzling three-quarter moon. Rather than park in front of Leticia's, I park in front of the house next door so I'll have a view of the back where Zachary says we'll have access. I scan Leticia's house. With dormer windows, a split roof with gently sloping eaves, and a broad front porch, I estimate it was built in the forties and considered quite nice at the time. These days the porch rail has collapsed and been left in its crippled position. And the dormers are boarded over. There's a detached one-car garage in the back corner of the lot and the driveway has been widened by replacing a section of lawn (weeds) with cement. The driveway holds six cars; the two nearest the garage rest on blocks. The cars are unattractive, dented old boxes, definitely not vehicles that attract collectors. Yet there they are, a collection. The wall between the cars and

< 116 >

the house is lined with tall narrow structures – refrigerators. I count eight of them.

In the last couple of weeks I've learned that people collect all kinds of things, though their reasons escape me. Is it based on the premise that if having one of a thing is nice, having a dozen must be a dozen times nicer? Completely irrational. And collecting old refrigerators? My curiosity kicks in. If she's got this much useless stuff outside the house, what does she have inside? I'm going to tell Zachary that I'll do it.

I forgot to check and see if Wally was following me when I left work. I've been parked for almost five minutes before I notice the outline of a police car parked half a block behind me. Damn it.

When I get home the lights are on but Mom's nowhere to be found. Not out back or in the kitchen or in her room. I walk through the house calling her name. I go back out to the garage to see if her car's there, which just shows how spacey I am, because I pulled into the garage five minutes ago and honestly can't remember if it was there or not. It's right where it should be.

Before heading up to my room, I glance out the front window, scanning the shadows. Chloe said she'd be by to get her car, but it's still parked out there. The street light illuminates a profile in the driver's seat. I go out through the front door and join Mom in Chloe's car.

"What's going on?"

"I bought Chloe this car."

"Yes."

"Was that a police car that followed you home?"

"Has he gone?" I look all around, but fat-faced Wally Roach isn't in sight. "It's what happens when you're an addict. Local law enforcement gets to harass you."

< 117 >

"That man is keeping me from my grandchild."

"Give it time."

"Technically this car belongs to me. It's in my name."

"Don't even go there. It would just exacerbate."

"If I hold it hostage at least she'd have to talk to me. At least there would be communication."

"Or her new daddy would buy her a new one and you'd be out of the picture forever."

"Why do you think he's doing this? Is he that mad at me? Was what I did so horrible?"

"Maybe it's not about you. Maybe Chloe just wants to get to know her father. And maybe he wants to spend time with his daughter and his granddaughter. Sometimes people are exactly what they seem to be." He'd seemed like a well-meaning uncomplicated guy.

"This came today." She holds out a white A4 envelope.

"What is it?" It's too dark out here to read it.

"I'm being sued by the couple who was going to adopt. Interference with Contractual Relations."

"Wow. I don't have a clue what that means."

"They're saying I used my influence to stop the adoption."

"What are you going to do?" I'm not going to point out that this is absolutely what she did.

"Talk to a lawyer, I guess."

She sighs and we sit in silence for several minutes.

"What time do you have to be at work tomorrow?" she asks after a while.

"Noon."

"I want you to go to Aimes and check on Chloe and the baby."

"Money's tight and it's an hour away."

"I'll reimburse you for the gas."

"Okay."

< 118 >

I go up to my room. I haven't yet had a chance to research the items I pulled from the Meskar house, so I do that now. I slide them from beneath my bed, examine them, and then search the collectors' websites. Then I post the descriptions. When I check in the morning, I've had an offer of eight hundred for the silverware, two hundred for the Delft serving dish, and three hundred for the pair of Waterford vases. I grab a quick bite, a quick smoke with coffee, and head out.

My impression of Aimes when we were here last week was that it's basic and drab, the progeny of the union between hot wind and dry grit. To my surprise, there's actually a more affluent section of Aimes that we missed. It's absurd to think that a town this small has a suburb, but a mile off the highway, beyond the boundary marked by Wal-Mart and the medical building, a residential area rises out of the flat land.

An elegant façade, marked by a sign reading *PALO DURO ESTATES,* signals the entrance to the development where Henry Kearney lives. Having printed off the map, I roll through the gateway, take the right at the T-section, then the next left. The houses are larger here than in Aimes proper – two stories with double garages. Once again I find myself wondering – who lives here and why? Where do the people work when their little town seems to support no industry other than the DQ, a rural school, and a Wal-Mart? And is there tension between the people who live in these more expensive homes and the people who occupy the older homes in town?

On closer inspection, though, what I'm looking at is a cut-and-paste development. All the homes are variations of the same design. Some are red brick, some orange; some are trimmed in white, some in gray. Chloe's father's house

< 119 >

is just one of many – same elevated main entry, same two-story window that displays the interior stairs. I park on the street and ring the doorbell. Chloe answers immediately

"It took you long enough," she says, standing back to let me in. She carries Allison in a front-riding halter. All that's visible of my niece is a pink hat.

"I've been sent to check on you."

"No, you've been sent to get me the hell out of here."

She points her chin toward the area behind the door. Several items are piled there – a car seat, a bassinet, two packs of diapers, two suitcases full of whatever. She's packed and waiting.

"How did you know I was coming?"

"You think I don't know Mom? Hurry." She grabs one of the suitcases and heads out the door, saying over her shoulder, "He had a couple of early appointments, then he said he'd be home around nine to check on us. Meanwhile, I'm a prisoner with no way to go anywhere. He said he'd take me to get my car yesterday, but he kept making excuses."

I carry the car seat out to the car. She settles the baby in while I fetch the rest of her things. I make two trips and close the front door behind me. Well, this'll make Mom happy.

"So?" I ask as soon as we're on the highway. I'm irritated. She didn't give me even a minute to look around her dad's house. And I was curious, too. I want to know what dads eat and wear and collect.

"He was weird. He wanted me to go to church with him. He called me a blessing. He called Allison a gift from God. He prays every time he puts food in his mouth."

"A lot of people are religious."

"Not me. And he's got a list of completely random things you can't do. Don't flush solid waste in that bathroom.

< 120 >

Don't watch that TV station. Don't eat that cheese. Don't open that window."

"Have you decided to forgive Mom?"

"Look at me. No income, no future, and a baby to take care of. Whose fault is it, if not Mom's?"

Silly girl. Mom didn't get her pregnant.

"So what are you going to do?"

"I'm going to think really hard." We make the rest of the drive in silence. Presumably Chloe's thinking really hard.

< 121 >

The Hoarder's House

When I get to work, the atmosphere is tense. Because I clocked her out when she actually left work instead of giving her the extra hours she asked for, Karen is giving me the silent treatment. The air is thick with her anger. Her movements speak. She jerks, she slams, she stomps. When I come near her, she pushes out a disgusted grunt and stalks in the opposite direction. I try apologizing but she asks what it is I'm apologizing for. It's all very passive/aggressive.

Zachary shows up at around one o'clock. Sniffing the air, looking around like he's lost something, it takes him less than ten seconds to discern the hostility. Predictably, he adores someone else's conflict. He keeps asking what's going on and Karen and I keep denying that anything's going on at all.

And she gets even more riled when Zachary puts her on the schedule to close on Tuesday night. For some reason – probably having to do with the inherent complexity of dealing with twins – she specifically asked that she not work past seven this week. When she realizes it's because Zachary and I are involved in some mutual escapade, well, it's not just me she's mad at. By the time Zachary and I head out on Tuesday evening she's been so furious for so long that I'm afraid she's going to burst.

Because Cockroach Wally and his sidekick have started

< 122 >

following me in the evening Zachary instigates an elaborate scheme where he follows me home and parks way up by the back gate. We go inside for a few minutes, then he makes a show of exiting the gate while I crouch-sneak into his car in a way that can't be seen from the street, hunkering down in the back seat until we've made a clean getaway.

"Did it work?" I straighten and look out the back window. No one's following us.

We lied to Mom, telling her we were going to an art exhibit at the high school. It bothers me that there's still another hour before the sun goes down.

"Leticia's neighbors are going to see us walking around outside her house."

"They're in front of their televisions." Zachary is dressed completely in black – black shirt, black jeans, black boots, black Stetson. He's even wearing a black kerchief fastened at the throat with an onyx bolo clasp. His B&E costume. Oh no, the neighbors won't notice us at all.

He parks around the corner from his cousin's street and we walk the half-block. One of her cars is gone, which I take as a sign that Zachary's right – she's not here. Attempting to look like we're supposed to be there, we amble up the driveway toward the back of the house.

"What's the deal with these refrigerators?" I ask, stopping between the cars and the white boxes.

"She's a hoarder."

Curious, I open one of them. It's completely packed with canned goods. Every shelf, row after row, tower upon tower. Beans, tomatoes, spinach, soup, tuna. I pluck a can of kidney beans from the top of one of the towers. It expired two years ago. Putting it back, I close this door and open the next in line. It too is full of cans. And the next, and the next. There must be two thousand cans. Maybe more.

< 123 >

"Olivia, get a move on." Zachary has gone around the corner of the house. I close the refrigerator and follow the sound of his voice. He's waiting on the elevated stoop, staring out over the backyard, which is full of all kinds of paraphernalia. Metal bed frames lean against the wall of the garage. Washing machines and dryers line up at the back property line, forming a fence of sorts. These, too, are propping up metal frames. Stretched out across the ground are old-fashioned T-shaped clothesline poles – I estimate thirty of them. A fat rat zips across one of the poles.

Zachary turns the knob of the back door and pushes it open. A bell jingles as he disappears inside. I follow and immediately bump into Zachary who is unable to advance further. Peering around him, I see that his way is blocked by a shoulder-high barrier constructed of furniture – a broad sideboard with dining chairs stacked on top of it. And the view through the chair legs presents more furniture, which all appears damaged – drawers with no knobs that won't fully close, splintered panels, cracked mirrors.

"We're going to have to close the door before we can go anywhere," he says.

I squeeze up against his back to make room for the arc of the door. Once again the bell jingles – an annoying sound. When the door's closed a narrow pathway opens to our right. Bookcases line both sides of the path, reaching to within a foot of the ceiling. The shelves are packed with more canned goods. Vision is murky because the shelving blocks the window.

"She must be seriously insecure about food," I say.

"It's just one of the things she collects. It's what hoarders do."

"It smells really bad." The odor is hot, sharp, and gamey. Critters are living in here.

< 124 >

"You don't have to come any further. All I need for you to do is to stay by the door and keep watch." He steps into the gloom.

Is he kidding? I've never seen anything like this and there's no way I'm missing it. I give him a few seconds' lead before I follow. I expect a maze, but really there's no choice but to follow the single path. There are no offshoots, no options. The stuff tells me where to go. The shelves turn left and I turn left. The objects change; now my way is lined with old bulky televisions. And when I come to the end of the TVs, the path goes right, into a hallway that's bordered with stacks of books, three deep on both sides, floor to ceiling, one end to the other, letting off at doorways. There appears to be no system, they're just stacked – large on small, children's on adults', hardbacks on paperbacks. The edge of a coffee table book pokes out, forming a ledge. A cockroach perches there, antennae on alert as it surveys its domain.

Zachary is a shadow in the room at the end of the hall. I'm completely turned around. From the outside this place looks small, incapable of holding all this stuff. But right now I couldn't tell you which direction is the street and which is the back. I pause at every door. The bathroom's so cluttered that the walls aren't visible. The countertop is piled high with empty busted picture frames. The tub is full of swords – lethal ancient rusty swords. Candles are piled on the closed toilet seat, the toilet lid, and the floor all around the toilet. Every item in the room is coated with greasy gray fuzz.

The next room I enter holds kitchen items – bins full of warped spatulas, bins full of stained potholders, bins full of rusty can openers. There's a mountain of lidless plastic containers and another mountain of plastic lids sans

< 125 >

containers. Give-away plastic cups form columns and the columns form walls. There's not an area of the room that isn't stacked high. A table holds mixing bowls of every kind – Pyrex, metal, Corning. I count six sets of colorful nesting bowls, circa 1950. A complete set of these mixing bowls in good condition is worth a couple of hundred dollars. The area beneath the table is filled with more bowls.

Because I'm trying to figure out a way to get the bowls out of here without Zachary noticing, it takes a few seconds for the distant jingling to register – but when I figure it out, I fly from the room and down the hall to Zachary. For a second I take in the room's contents – lamps, electric fans, ironing boards. Zachary's on his hands and knees in the closet, pushing boxes around and muttering about the smell and the mold.

"She's home!" My hissing whisper is hysterical. This wasn't supposed to happen. "I just heard the bell on the back door."

"I thought you were keeping watch." Terror, accusation, disgust – his glare says it all.

"What good would that have done? What are we going to do?" For the first time in months my heart is actually going full speed, thumping hard. I'm not used to it and it doesn't feel good or right.

"Quick! Get in here."

I step into the closet and he closes the door. And that's how we end up sitting in a dark filthy closet for three hours.

< 126 >

Bats in Flight

Leticia's a whistler. At one point thready strains of *How Great Thou Art* enter the room outside our closet, then the melody fades as she moves away. During this waiting time Zachary doggedly continues his search, peering into musty boxes from behind the tiny flashlight that's hooked on his key chain. I'm happy for him when he comes across the carton containing the family documents. It's eleven when we realize Leticia's been quiet for a while and it's safe to leave. The box is heavier than we thought it would be and we haul it between us. In places that are narrow, Zachary walks backwards. We stupidly forget the bell on the back door and when it ding-a-lings above our heads, panic sends us racing through the backyard, tripping and hopping over the clotheslines poles with our shared burden, and taking cover on the far side of the garage.

She must be a sound sleeper because there's no reaction from inside. After a few minutes we come out of hiding and make our way around the block to the car.

"We forgot to close her back door," Zachary says.

"Leave it. No one's going in there."

"She's my cousin." He gets out of the car and walks away. Five minutes later he's back.

"Why do you think she hoards things?" I ask as soon as he's settled behind the wheel.

< 127 >

"I suppose it's because she identifies with useless stuff," he responds.

"She's sick. She needs help."

"I wonder why she came home early. Probably rehearsal got cancelled for some reason. Thanks for going with me."

See? I did Zachary a favor. I do things for others. I'm not all about only doing for myself. It was an interesting adventure. I wish I'd had more time in there. I wish I could have grabbed those bowls.

Sleep is an unpleasant tangle of sheets, so I get up as soon as I hear Mom moving around downstairs. Even though it's her day off, she's up at her regular time. Together we stand at the front window and watch the dog sniff, sneeze, and do his business. To my surprise, when he drifts from our yard, Mom slips on her sandals and heads toward the door.

"Where are you going?"

"I'm going to see where he lives."

"I'll come."

The dog wanders in and out of the shadows, lifting his leg at trees and curbs and mailboxes. Mom and I follow along out in the street, keeping an eye on him. A few of the houses have lights on, but most are still dark. It's only five forty-five.

"This is the best time of day," I say.

"I've always thought so."

"Why does Zachary live in Caprock? Why isn't he in Los Angeles or New York?"

"Contrary to what you believe, Caprock isn't hell."

"He doesn't fit in here. And the store in the mall makes absolutely nothing."

"He moved to Santa Fe for a few years in the eighties. When he moved back home, something seemed off."

"Off?"

< 128 >

"He was quieter, seemed to take his work more seriously. I asked, but he wouldn't talk."

"You think someone broke his heart?"

"Or maybe his pride took a hit. He's a proud man." The sun's not up but the eastern sky is growing pale. "But whatever it was, he got over it. He's happy here. Why does that bother you?"

"Because he's gifted. He belongs in a sparkling pulsating city, not a torpid northwest Texas town."

"A pulsating city sounds exhausting."

The dog stops on the porch of the house on the corner. The door opens a crack, a fan of light leaks out, the dog goes in, and the door closes.

"Now we know," Mom says.

"Now we know," I echo.

When we get home Chloe's sitting at the kitchen table nursing Allison. I'm having a hard time getting used to the idea of my sister with a baby. Chloe looks sleepy and content until Mom speaks – then her jaw firms and her brows furrow. Not only has there been no forgiveness, there hasn't even been a slight letting up. Chloe is set hard, hard, hard against Mom.

"Chloe, you and Allison have an appointment with the pediatrician at ten." Mom's so afraid of inciting that her voice has no inflection at all.

"Olivia, tell her I'm aware."

This has been going on since Chloe brought the baby home. Mom addresses Chloe directly, and Chloe ricochets information and complaints off me like I'm a backboard. I'm sure it'll become tedious at some point, but so far it's keeping me amused.

"Mom, she's aware," I say.

"I'm right here, Olivia. I heard what she said."

< 129 >

"Olivia, tell her that if she actually heard something I said, it'd be a first."

"Mom," I obey, "she seems to think you don't listen when she speaks."

"Oh good God." Mom throws up her hands in exasperation and stalks from the kitchen.

"This can't go on much longer," I say to my bratty little sister.

"It can go on for as long as I want it to."

Another thing that's happened since Chloe had her baby is that Mom has become hyper-vigilant concerning my whereabouts and activities. She calls me every twenty minutes. She shows up at work at odd times. She checks with Jane or Zachary to make sure I'm where I say I'll be. Taking on the role of therapist, I've concluded that because she's lost control in her relationship with Chloe, she's determined not to let me get the upper hand. My plan is to be absolutely perfect until she calms down. The result is that not only have I been unable to package and send the Meskar items, I haven't been able to get by the bank to fill out a deposit slip for the payments. Also, I haven't been able to get out to the drive-in to get the gumball machine. I hoped I could get to these things this morning. But now, at ten-thirty, there's no way that's going to happen.

My appointment with the cardiologist was at eight-thirty. I was here but he wasn't. He never is. I've got to be at work at noon. The waiting room seats a dozen people and every seat is taken. I was the first appointment and I'm paranoid that when the doctor arrives he'll take one of the other people first. It's happened before. The others in the room are all older than I am – in their sixties and seventies. Occasionally a chubby woman in blue scrubs opens the door that leads to the exam rooms, pokes her head out,

< 130 >

and calls a name. That person rises, disappears through the door, and is led through a carpeted maze and shown into a room. He or she takes off his shirt or opens her blouse, the sensors are placed, and the EKG is taken. Then the patient is escorted back to the waiting room to wait and wait and wait.

Finally there's a flurry behind the glass window. The doctor has arrived. Ten minutes later my name is called and I'm once again invited beyond the sacred door.

Doctor Ramirez is in his mid-fifties. Rotund, gray, too busy to look a person in the eye. He glances up from my EKG when I enter, then looks quickly back down.

"Sorry about the delay." At least he apologizes. Most don't. He returns his attention to the pattern in front of him. After a minute he says, "Everything looks good. Any problems?"

"I was wondering if maybe it wasn't time for a little exercise. Some yoga, maybe."

"Walking only. Half an hour daily, no more just yet. Don't get overheated or dehydrated."

He stands and offers his hand for a farewell shake. Two hours of waiting for a three-minute consultation. Another price I have to pay.

But at least I have time to stop by the UPS store to get the packages sent. And I get by the bank, which means thirteen hundred more in my account.

That evening Mom and Chloe and I – plus Allison – are hanging out on the back porch. We're a gloomy group. Chloe's still not talking to Mom and Mom is pretending she doesn't care. It occurs to me that I know something interesting we can do.

"Come on," I say. "Let's go for a drive. It'll only take an hour or so."

< 131 >

We load the car seat and the baby in the back. Chloe slides in next to Allison, Mom plops into shotgun, and in half an hour I turn on to the dirt road that borders the Meskar property and pull to a stop at the verge.

"What are we doing here?" Mom's grumpy and trying not to show it. But her grunts and huffs are telling.

"Just watch," I tell her, pointing toward the house.

Usually it would be unbearable to peer in that direction at this time of day because the western sun can be fierce. But this evening the sunset is filtered through clouds, casting split beams of yellow, peach, pink, and violet.

"It's a lovely sunset." Mom's voice is wistful, as though this sunset reminds her of another.

A few seconds later bats start flying from the Meskar garage. Just a few at first. Then a few more. Then several hundred. An undulating funnel forms above the structure, whirling and pulsing and black, a tornado made of bats. Then they break formation and disperse in a disorganized flurry.

In less than a minute there's not a bat in sight.

"That was wonderful," Mom says. "How did you know?"

"Someone at the mall mentioned it."

"He keeps calling and coming by." This from Chloe who, so far, has been a silent lump.

Mom and I turn in our seats and look at her.

"Who?" Mom asks. "Allison's father?"

"No, mine. My father. Henry," Chloe tells her. "He says he wants me to come home, as if that house out there is where I've lived all my life. He says he wants to help with Allison."

"What were you looking for when you contacted him?" It's not a told-you-so voice. Mom genuinely wants to know.

"Well, I guess I hoped he'd help out financially. But it's

< 132 >

turned out that it's not me wanting something from him, it's him wanting something from me."

"You haven't lost your life, you know. You've got options."

"Name one."

"You could live at home and do your senior year at Pan UT. And as far as med school, you'd definitely qualify for grants and scholarships. And you could take out a loan for the rest."

"I'd owe a fortune when I got out."

"So? You'd be like millions of other people. I know it's not the way you planned on doing it, but it's a small detour, that's all."

For the first time since deciding to keep her baby, Chloe looks hopeful.

< 133 >

Chloe's Dad

I'm optimistic about finding a buyer for the gumball machine. There are two people who've shown an interest – a man in Alabama and a woman in Nevada. The man is a collector and the woman owns a novelty shop which, I see from her website, specializes in antique cutesy items like Bakelite phones and box cameras. A gumball machine would fit right in.

I go through the routine again – the drive to the country, the loud boom box, kerosene, WD-40. It takes two hours of intense hunched labor and another skinned knuckle to free the base. And it's too heavy to lift; I end up getting it out of there by wrapping my arms around its big spherical head and dragging it across the cement floor. The scraping noise is painful.

My straining arms are full of the gumball machine when I hear the rattler. Bent beneath the weight of the iron stand, poised with the heavy thing halfway between the ground and the trunk of my car, I react without thought, dumping the bubble gum machine into the trunk and leaping backward. I trip over my feet and fall flat on my rear end.

From this angle I have a good view of the snake, which is coiled right beneath the rear of the car, inches away from where I just stood, its mouth opened and its venomous fangs bared. I can see the inside of its wet pink mouth.

< 134 >

I can see the rattle on its tail vibrating. I scramble back, crab-walking until my head bumps the building. My heart is speed-stomping in my chest. I can feel it in my ears.

"Asshole," I say as much to myself as to the snake. Pushing myself up the wall and making a wide wary circle to the driver's door, I leap in, turn the key, and drive away, trunk lid bouncing as I bump thirty yards toward the exit before stopping and getting out of the car to check on my new treasure. Fearing that being so carelessly tossed like that might have broken it, I check it carefully. Luck was with me on this one. It's fine; I'm fine. I look back toward the building. I've left the door wide open. The snake isn't in sight. I close the trunk and head home. I've had it with this place. I won't be coming back out here and I'm not going to think anymore about the pinball machine. It'll just have to stay here forever.

I'm halfway back to Caprock when my phone rings. Expecting Mom, I don't bother to check the caller ID. To my surprise, a male voice asks for me.

"This is Olivia."

"Olivia, it's Henry. Henry Kearney."

Chloe's father, small town dermatologist and man of prayer. A delicious wave of curiosity washes through my system.

"Hi, Henry. What can I do for you?"

"Meet me. For coffee. You work at the mall, right? Are you free during your break?"

My first thought is that my break is when I step out into the blazing sun and draw hot detrimental smoke into my lungs. That's what break is for. But knowing Zachary, he'll grant me some extra time this afternoon if I promise to deliver the scoop.

"Sure. Two forty-five at Java Jean's in the food court."

< 135 >

"Thank you. Good. See you then." And he ends the call.

As anticipated, Zachary's thrilled at the notion of me meeting Chloe's dad.

"I just don't know what's going on with your family," he says. "You were all so boring for years and years. And now every time I turn around there's some unexpected development."

"When you have twins something unexpected's always happening." This from Karen, whose anger has finally dissipated, which means she's once again going on about the unique complications of twinship.

At two forty-five I stroll toward Java Jean's. Henry Kearney is sitting in the corner booth, just inside the short barrier that encircles the coffee shop, which gives him a broad view of both the food court and the mall. I get a small coffee and join him. A man of old-fashioned manners, he stands when he sees me approaching. Every time I've seen him he's been dressed in khakis, a golf shirt, and loafers. On the table in front of him is a fruit drink of some kind.

"Hi, Henry. I was surprised you called." I pull the chair out, sit, and remove the lid from my coffee. The warm aroma makes me long for a cigarette.

"How're Chloe and Allison?" he asks.

He sits back down as soon as I'm seated. Here's one of the things I know that people who never leave this part of the world don't – men in other places do not stand when a woman approaches or rises from her seat.

"They're fine," I tell him. "I don't know much about babies, but Allison seems to be an exceptionally cooperative one."

On the mall side of the rail, Zachary walks by our table. His head is tilted at a contemplative angle as he pretends to ponder heavy concerns. He strolls past, then comes to a full

< 136 >

stop, lifts his head, and takes a good long look at Henry. Then, curiosity satisfied, he sends me a wave and a smirk, before turning back toward the store.

"What can I do for you, Henry?"

"She doesn't answer when I call. She doesn't open the door when I go by the house." His wide-open eyes reflect distress that's just a bit too fervent. "I never knew she existed – and now that I know, is it so wrong of me to want to get to know her?"

"She's going through a tough time right now." I wonder how it is that this guy has so much free time. Don't the folks in Aimes need their dermatologist?

"One of my biggest regrets has always been that I never had children. And now I find out I've had a daughter this whole time." The fine tremor in his fingers and the clench of his jaw signal his anger. He continues, "I'm furious, just plain furious. How could she have kept something like this from me?"

It takes me a second to catch up – he's talking about Mom, not Chloe. I guess he's not used to Mom the way I am. It would never have occurred to her that what she did was in any way unfair or cruel. He was married at the time. He moved away soon after. It's not like he ever checked to see if she was pregnant after their quickie in the supply closet (or wherever). She had a baby; she took care of it. If she'd told him, he might have wanted to be involved in Chloe's life, which meant that he'd be a presence forever. And Mom definitely didn't want that – so yeah, what she did was selfish. But we're all selfish in our own ways, pretty much daily.

"Why would she contact me and then not want to see me?" Now he's talking about Chloe. "Why would she ask me to take her and her baby into my home and then sneak off without saying good-bye?"

< 137 >

"Maybe you should dial it back," I tell him. "Let her come to you."

"What if she never does?" He releases a sigh. "I know she's broke and scared. I offered to help with expenses. All I ask in return is that she gets to know me and lets me get to know her."

"She's overwhelmed. Not only has she taken on the responsibility for a baby, now you're making demands, too."

"I want you to talk to her for me."

"What would you have me say?"

"Tell her that this is new to me, too. Tell her that I'm a good man. And that I want to be the father she needs."

"Okay," I agree, but it's not okay. He wants me to say these things when I don't even know him. Replacing the lid on the remainder of my coffee, I stand. It's time for the second part of my break.

"Thanks for meeting me." He, too, stands, holding out his hand for a shake. I accept his hand knowing that he thinks we're sealing some kind of deal, which is absolutely not the case.

"No problem." I slide a few inches toward the exit. But he's a hand holder. He presses my hand between both of his palms and looks deeply into my eyes as though trying to see my thoughts. When he finally releases my hand I turn away, moving quickly. By the time I reach the mall exit, I'm practically running, trying to escape the whisper of my powdery friend who, from behind the locked door in my mind, emits a seductive hiss – *let me out, you want me, you need me, you know you do.*

Oh, I do, I do. If I had any connections in this town I'd be on the phone. I'd beg. I'd promise anything.

The hot outside air surrounds me, penetrating to my marrow. Concentrating on the heat, my fingers tremble as I

< 138 >

extract a cigarette and my lighter. I aim my feet toward the designated area. Inhale. Exhale. Aah. It's not cocaine, but it offers a tiny fraction of relief.

When I return to the store Zachary's waiting for a report.

"Well?" he asks. "What do you think? What did he want?"

"I don't get the guy," I say. "Everything's exaggerated with him. Like, he's interested in Chloe's well-being, but weirdly, he's too interested. And I guess I could see him being put out with Mom, but he's not just put out, he's furious. That was his word – furious."

"Hmm. Maybe dermatologists are strange." Typical of Zachary – a conclusion that has nothing to do with anything.

At six Karen rushes off to feed her family. Zachary leaves to fetch take-out from Pei Wei and deliver it to Mom and Chloe. And I'm left to close the store. I'm feeling itchy and discontent and I don't know why. The meeting with Henry left me unsettled. I don't understand his motives, and his intensity bothered me. On the flipside, it perturbs me that I'm so suspicious. He obviously cares about my sister. What's wrong with me that I can't accept that some people are simply what they appear to be? Henry is most likely a kind person who wants to help. Maybe I should try harder to appreciate the good in people instead of looking for the bad bits of myself in everyone.

With that in mind, I vow to be more charitable in my thoughts – and looky here; Wally Roach, the most annoying person on the planet, is out in the mall, sauntering my way. This is a perfect opportunity to try out my new, more open-minded, philosophy.

"Hey, Wally," I greet. "Where's your partner this evening?"

"Food court." Right away he claims a corner of the

< 139 >

counter, resting his forearm across the top of the glass case. It'll leave an oily smudge on the glass, which I'll rush to clean as soon as he's out of here.

"What can I do for you?"

"In high school you always thought you were better than everybody else, and now look at you, a counter girl in the mall, living with your mom and attending addiction meetings."

Maybe Wally isn't the place to begin exercising tolerance.

"Why have you been following me?" I ask.

"I heard your little sister had a baby, no husband in sight."

"You heard right."

"One of them lesbian households."

"Huh?"

"Lesbians. You want the babies but not the men." He sneers. I can see the white of his T-shirt where his belly strains the front buttons of his dark uniform. His shiny head reflects the overhead lights.

"Why are you here?"

"Just checking on you, like I said I would."

"Well, isn't that kind of you."

"And don't you forget it." With that he turns and leaves the store. His heavy-man swagger carries him away at too slow a pace.

That night when I get home Mom is sitting in the dark on the back porch by herself.

"How's it going?" I ask, collapsing into my chair.

"I collected all the dog mess in a garbage bag and I'm fixing to dump it on that idiot's lawn."

"I'll go with you," I offer.

With Mom wearing rubber gloves and strangling her stinky trash bag, we take a relaxed walk to the house on the corner.

< 140 >

I wait out on the sidewalk as she starts at the front of the house and systematically distributes her load from there to where I'm standing.

As we head home Wally pulls up beside us and lowers his window. Great. Now he's going to arrest us for vandalism.

"What did you just do?" he asks. The interior of the car is in shadow. All I can see of his partner is her silhouette as she leans toward us.

"Those people's dog has been doing his business in our yard," I tell him. "We gave it back to them."

"Oh. Okay then." Raising his window he drives away.

< 141 >

I Cross a Line

This is a New Testament morning. Acts 2:2.

And suddenly there came from heaven a noise like a violent rushing wind, and it filled the whole house where they were sitting.

Pentecost. The arrival of the Holy Spirit. I think it would have been cool to have been there. Wind from heaven, tongues of fire, people speaking languages they'd never learned. Life-altering. An experience that would change everything you thought you knew and would influence every action you took from that moment on. Modern religion seems so flat. No passion, no miracles, no amazing manifestations.

When I get downstairs Mom's already gone to work and Chloe's sitting at the kitchen table with Allison's tiny mouth fastened to her breast. Papers are spread all over the table. Transfer forms, scholarship information, government loan applications, single-parent benefit advisories.

"Mom's gonna wear out the printer," I say.

"Please tell me my life isn't over."

"Your life isn't over."

"Maybe I should do what you do when you feel trapped – have a secret life full of clandestine adventures."

"Chloe Henderson, full-time mother, full-time student. And hey, in her spare time she fights crime."

< 142 >

"Or spies for the government."

"How do you see Henry Kearney fitting into this exciting life of yours?"

"He wanted to move too fast." She sighs as she changes the baby from one breast to the other. "He wanted to add an extra room to his house for Allison and me. He was all excited because there's a childcare facility in his building. Childcare so I could do what? – work at the Dairy Queen? I've got my senior year to finish."

"You're not planning on giving him any time at all?"

"It can't be up to me to solve his loneliness issues."

"Maybe a weekend every once in a while, just to get to know him?"

"He thinks everything that happens is God's will. As though every mistake we make is because some higher power is in charge of our actions. Like God willed me to get pregnant."

"I don't know what to say to that." I take my coffee out to the porch so I can have a cigarette. When I come back in she and the baby have gone upstairs.

I haven't been able to stop thinking about Zachary's cousin's house. I'm curious about what kind of person lives like that. During the night every time I slipped into the lightest doze my mind was taken over by images of sky-high clutter. It depresses me that such a place exists. And it disturbs me that Zachary is so unconcerned. Also, I want those bowls. It can't hurt to get a deeper feel for the situation, so I stop by her house on the way to my appointment with Jane.

She answers the door wearing purple sweat pants and a faded turquoise T-shirt. Here is a woman who doesn't care about creating an impression. Old computer screens form an eerie wall beyond her shoulder. The heavy rotten odor of the place drifts out.

< 143 >

"What can I do for you?" She's got a sweet face – turned-up nose, welcoming smile.

"I'm collecting items for a charity kitchen our church is opening on Humble Road," I say, enjoying the fabrication. "We particularly need utensils and mixing bowls."

"Oh, no." Her smile disappears, and her eyes grow flat and hard. "I don't have anything like that." She closes the door. So now I know.

Fifteen minutes later I'm in Jane's office, sitting in my usual spot. Today she's wearing a dress instead of one of her twin sets. A horrible choice. She's short and carries extra weight in her mid-section, and there are knife pleats at every seam – at the shoulder, at the waist, descending from the yoke at the back. Though the cerulean looks good with her skin tone, the excess fabric makes her look like a giant blueberry.

"What do you know about hoarding?" I ask.

"Only what I've seen on reality shows. I find it both horrifying and fascinating."

"What causes it? It's a sickness, right?"

"Any number of neuroses could be involved. Why are you asking me this?"

"Zachary's cousin is a hoarder."

"Really? We have a hoarder right here in Caprock?" She leans forward in her chair, clearly interested.

"Yeah, I was curious so I drove by her house." I can't tell Jane the truth about anything. "Old cars in the driveway, a whole line of refrigerators beside the house, washers and dryers in the back – and that's just the outside."

"Wow. I'd give anything – " Halting mid-sentence, she gives a little shake before refocusing. "I can't help but wonder why you'd drive by the home of a complete stranger and take inventory."

< 144 >

"You'd give anything to what, Jane?"

"Nothing. Never mind."

"Why can't you just admit that you're curious?" She's been distant and condescending ever since I got back to Caprock. "You know what? I'm fed up with you acting like we don't know each other. I'm tired of you being so clinical about what I'm going through. And I'm tired of you pretending you're something you're not – like you don't get a kick out of the crazy things people do, when you're every bit as curious as I am about that woman whose house is so stacked high with useless stuff that she can't even get to her toilet!" A gesture seems called for so, indignant and caught up in my drama, I rise from my chair and stomp toward the door.

"Stop right there."

Hand on the knob, I stop. As disgusted as I am with this whole situation, it's of my own making and I know the game I have to play. I can't pick up the reins of my life until Jane signs off. I turn back, making no attempt to conceal my resentment. Returning to my seat, I drop into it with the exaggerated angst of a spoiled thirteen-year-old.

"Can't get to her toilet, that's what you said. You've been in there." She's trying for somber disapproval, but her furrowed brow can't disguise her interest.

I don't reveal and I don't deny.

"You've been inside that hoarder's house," she says again. "You knocked on her door and she let you in. Why would you go there? What was it like?"

Once again I don't respond. I have no patience with someone who wants to know without seeing for herself, someone who wants to experience but won't commit. After a few seconds of silence she moves on to other subjects. I've received one thing from this session that I wasn't looking

< 145 >

for, but badly need – an ego boost. For the first time in a long time I feel special and maybe a little superior. Because I choose adventures and take the initiative. Because I see for myself while Jane sits on her padded backside and wonders.

The best offer for the gumball machine is from the man in Alabama – three-fifty when I hoped to get four. But the buyer's paying for shipping, which puts his cost over the standard price, so I'm okay with the loss.

In the middle of the night I'm wide awake and exhausted from hours of flipping from one side to the other. Insignificant scenes, wrapped in drowsiness, flow through my mind. I remember the morning noises of the rehab facility in Dallas – pings and squeaks and groaning yawns. And then the setting changes and I'm imagining a silver Mercedes parked in front of the house. It feels like I've seen it out there recently without really noticing. Chloe's dad's car? Maybe. Chloe said he's been coming by the house. And he, too, mentioned that he's been coming by. Sometimes my mind plays with time. Maybe it was out there yesterday or the day before. Or maybe I'm remembering it parked out there when he first came by.

Realizing that I'm never going to get to sleep, I throw the covers aside and pull on jeans and a T-shirt. I'm going for a drive. The streets are empty and quiet. I feel like I'm the only person awake in the whole city. Even Wally Roach isn't cruising. Before I know it I'm driving around and around Zachary's cousin's block. I know why I'm here, but I don't want to know. Without admitting that my actions are mine, without owning my intentions, I come to a stop in front of her house, get out of the car, and run on tiptoes up her driveway.

I remember the bell on the back door. It hangs at the top of the jamb and all it takes to muffle it is to reach up and

< 146 >

take hold of it before it drops down from the door being opened.

I know my way to the bowls. There are two bedrooms further down the hallway that I didn't go into the other day and Leticia is asleep in one of them. I imagine her in bed. Instead of sheets and blankets she sleeps under a hill made of her collections – old towels and worn-out pillows and ragged doilies. Around her bed are mountains of empty milk cartons and splintered wicker baskets. Following the walls of canned goods and TVs to the room where the kitchenware is kept, I grab one set of the nesting bowls and carry it to the back door. Then I return for another set. And then a third.

I transfer the bowls from inside the door to the back porch one set at a time, catching the bell each time to keep it silent. When I'm outside and the door is closed I stack the bowl sets on top of each other, filling my arms. Then I carry them to the car and carefully place them in the floorboard of the back seat. I get in my car and drive away.

< 147 >

We Aren't Friends

Ten years ago I would have said my life was marked by boundaries I simply would not cross. The me of back then would have arrogantly, adamantly insisted that I'd never cross the line between occasional use and addiction. That me would never have neglected payment of money owed.

Entering someone's house while they were asleep, and helping myself to their possessions, would have been so far out of my realm of acceptable behavior that the notion would never have entered my mind. What happened to my younger self? Where did my scruples go, and why?

Maybe the reason for my adherence to the rules was more out of fear of getting caught than any actual moral code – and now, having crossed the line that marks the wrong side of the law, fear is no longer a deterrent. Also, I have a gift for rationalization: she won't even notice the bowls are gone; she would never have used them; in her care, their value would never have been realized. I, on the other hand, have already found buyers for them, and I will put the money they bring in to good use.

And speaking of the law, I've been notified that my records have finally followed me from Dallas and that a local parole officer has been assigned to my case. Officer Ariana Smoot. I have an appointment with her this morning. Though somewhat curious about what a Caprock

< 148 >

parole officer looks like and what hoops she'll expect me to jump through, I'm resentful that this new obligation has entered the picture. As anticipated, a collector snapped up the bowls within an hour; two hundred and fifty a set, and I want to send them off. Also, the bubble gum machine is packed and ready to ship. But instead of taking care of business, I've got to meet with my parole officer.

So it's understandable that when I arrive at Officer Smoot's door, I'm feeling truculent. My knock is impatient and I count the seconds it takes for her to respond. But when she opens the door all it takes is the sight of her to lift my spirits. She's wearing the exact same dress Jane wore yesterday.

The giant blueberry dress. And it looks every bit as bad on her as it did on Jane. Like Jane, she's too short to carry off all the pleats and, with ginger hair and green eyes, the unrelieved blue enhances her freckles and makes her look pasty. She greets me with a limp handshake, invites me into her office, and hands me papers – two forms to fill out, a list of parole rules, her contact information, and a schedule of meetings. I'm already aware of most of the requirements – join a support group, follow the twelve steps (really only six), get a job, attend regular counseling sessions.

"I'm already doing all this stuff," I tell her, mourning the loss of the hour it's going to take to go over things I already know.

"I see from the record of your progress that you're keeping a journal."

"You discuss me with my therapist?"

"We consult, yes." I thought this was against all the rules of therapy. Apparently not if the therapy is court-mandated.

"Do you mind if I ask where you bought your dress?"

"We aren't friends, Olivia. We don't discuss clothes

< 149 >

or exchange recipes. I ask the questions and you stick to the guidelines and stay out of trouble. That's the way this works." Her features are small and tight and her lips are puckery, as though permanently set in the pronunciation of her last name – Smoot.

"I'm thrilled to have another indifferent person poke her nose in," I tell her.

"Don't get snippy. We meet here, at this same time, once a week. If there's ever a conflict, you discuss it with me. If you don't show up without telling me why, I will send a patrol car to your house. And I want you to start sending me your journal entries."

"You're giving me homework?" Jane never asked this of me.

"It'll give me a feel for how you're doing."

"I bet you don't make your other parolees do it," I say, knowing that I can't put my real life in a journal. I'll have to make it up.

"It's not too much to ask of someone with an advanced degree in journalism."

I leave her office feeling sorry for myself. The good thing is, the meeting that was scheduled to last an hour only lasted half that, so, though it means arriving at work ten minutes late, I'm able to get the items shipped. After I clock in I complain to Karen.

"I've already got too much stuff to do, and now my parole officer expects me to keep a daily journal."

"You don't know what busy is until you have twins," she says, leaning on the counter and staring out at the mall.

I'm at the computer going through the abandoned building photo website. There's an old school forty miles west of Caprock, in a town called Owensville. I've never heard of Owensville, which is surprising, considering its proximity.

< 150 >

The red brick school building in the picture looks like it's in pretty good shape. A wide set of stairs and columns mark an elevated frontage, giving the impression of space, bringing to mind school days in the 1940s. The bell tower rising from the left side of the building is counterbalanced by an impressively solid flagpole on the right. Though the roof is ragged and the windows all seem to be broken, it's an old-fashioned structure, gracious and interesting. No time to get out there tomorrow, but maybe the day after.

Determined to get it out of the way, I open the writing program on the computer and type out my first journal entry. Here's what I come up with:

Nothing much goes on at work. Our designs are expensive and unique, all created by Zachary Palin, my boss and a family friend. Occasionally customers will wander in, but our prices soon scare them back out the door. Karen, my co-worker, is the mother of twin girls and that's all she talks about. Zachary recently acquired some family documents that he's wanted for a long time, so that's a major event in his life. I recently had a disconcerting run-in with a rattlesnake and my little sister had a baby. Nothing else to say.

The single paragraph takes less than five minutes to write. I attach and send it. This is all the effort Ariana Smoot ("We aren't friends, Olivia.") is going to get. When the phone rings I jump to answer it.

"Palin Jewelry, how may I help you?"

"Olivia?" It's a man's voice. I'm wary – other than Zachary, there are no deep voices in my life.

"Yes?"

"Do you know where Geraldine is?"

Now I recognize the voice. Vernon, Geraldine's boy-friend. When she called asking me to pay back the money I borrowed, she mentioned they'd broken up. And here's

< 151 >

a life truth I'm learning: The powers-that-be can declare all kinds of rules about a recovering addict not being in contact with old friends, but the old life keeps showing up and there's not a lot a person can do to keep it from happening.

"I haven't seen her, but she called a while back," I tell him. "She said the two of you split up. How're you doing?"

"I need to find her. She's got something of mine."

Ominous. And intriguing. Vernon takes himself way too seriously. His menacing growl reminds me why I enjoyed hanging out with them. There was always something edgy going on. Drug deals gone sideways, violent ex-spouses showing up, some relative being indicted.

"She wanted the thirteen hundred I owed from when you guys helped me out, and when I said I didn't have it, she hung up."

"Here's news for you, Olivia – people don't like it when you borrow money and don't pay it back. They tend to get mad."

His voice is mean and there's no doubt he's issuing a threat. I don't like the ugly turn this is taking. I've seen Vernon go from charming to scary in a matter of seconds. Also, I have the feeling he'd forgotten about the money until I mentioned it. When will I learn to keep my mouth shut?

"I'll tell you the same thing I told her," I say. "I'm willing to pay. I can make fifty a month. That's the best I can do."

"I'm not a credit card company that takes payments. You owe the whole chunk."

"I'll see what I can work out." I'm just saying it to get him off the phone. It was Geraldine I considered a friend, not him.

"My address hasn't changed. Send it. And call me if she gets in touch again."

< 152 >

"Sure."

The line goes dead. How did he get this number? How did he find out where I work? Which one of them do I actually owe?

When I look up I'm shocked to see a familiar figure approaching the store. Geraldine. I'm beginning to think this mall in Caprock is like Times Square – if you stand here long enough every person you've ever known will pass by. Geraldine does not look good. Limping, dark hair going in all directions, clothes hanging crookedly. And as she draws closer, it becomes obvious that she has a black eye. Flinging a quick excuse over my shoulder, I rush out to head her off. The last thing I want is for Karen, judgmental and boringly respectable, to get a look at this loser who was once my friend.

< 153 >

The Owensville School Building

Three minutes later we're crouched over a table at the food court.

"You owe me," she says.

"You and everybody else."

Of course she's here about money. All around us people are calling to each other and settling plastic trays on tables. Geraldine has spilled a convoluted story about getting fired from her insurance job, borrowing money from her mother to pay rent, and then taking a few hundred dollars from Vernon's cash stash, even though they were no longer living together. She scratches at a rash on her neck with nervous fingers and her eyes don't seem to be able to settle on anything for longer than a couple of seconds.

"You broke into his house and took his money?" I'm appalled. Vernon's got a temper. And though he never hit her when they were a couple, I suspected this was because she always did what he told her to. She hasn't said, but I'm assuming he's the one who gave her the shiner.

"Technically it wasn't breaking," she says. "I still had a key. It was just to tide me over. And I took the car. Don't look at me like that – it's my car."

"He made the payments."

"It's in my name."

"But still."

< 154 >

"He was coming after me but Maya called and warned me."

"And the black eye?"

"Another guy, another night. A mistake."

Ugly and dramatic, just like old times. I'm pretty sure she's on something, not cocaine. Her pupils are tiny glittery points and her head keeps falling to the side like she can't control it. So it's not just about money, it's about money for drugs, which is something I absolutely can't get caught up in. I look around guiltily. Sitting here with her is against all the rules I've been living by for the last few months. And she's drawing attention – bruised eye, tangled hair, dressed all in red with her sleeve ripped at the shoulder so that her bra strap shows black against her deathly white skin. What the hell am I supposed to do with her?

"I'll get you the money tomorrow," I tell her. "But only half. Vernon gets his share." The last thing I need is him coming after me like he was coming after her. Pushing myself from the table I take a step away, but her bitter voice stops me.

"That's it? I'm your friend and I'm in trouble and that's all you've got?"

Reluctantly, I turn back.

"I can give you the number of the drug abuse hotline." It's an insensitive thing to say, but look at her. Unemployed, beat up, in need of cash for a fix. Did I once think her life was exciting? This was a woman I hung with and liked?

She responds with a sneer and a hiss.

"What do you want from me?" I ask. "We used to have fun together and I miss that. But I nearly died. I can't live that life anymore. What I can do is pay you what I owe you, which I will do tomorrow."

"You've changed," she tells me.

< 155 >

"I don't know that I have," I reply, thinking that the difference between me now and me then isn't what I was, but how I acted. On the surface I was fun and charming, supporting and sympathetic; but I still took care of myself first, just like I'm doing now. It's not a flattering thing to admit, but at least I know who I am, which is more than can be said about her.

"I need a place to stay," she says.

All I have in my wallet is enough for my next pack of cigarettes and she's not getting it.

"There are cheap hotels on the interstate."

"I don't have any money."

"What happened to what you took from Vernon?"

Her glance wanders downward, scanning her body as her fingers twitch.

"You can stay with me," I say.

I tell her I'll meet her outside the west exit around nine-fifteen. At nine I clock out, lock up, and hurry toward the east exit. Wally Roach and his partner are parked by my car and I give them a little wave. They follow me home and, with a little honk, drive away as soon as I pull into the garage. A door-to-door police escort. I wonder how long Geraldine will wait before she realizes I'm not going to show. Also, I wonder how naïve Wally is, to think that just because I go home means I'm going to stay there.

I manage a rough sleep for a couple of hours before coming fully awake. For once it's not my physical condition that disrupts my slumber – it's a crying baby. Allison sounds cranky. Poor Chloe. Kicking free from the tangle of sheets, I go down the hall and tap on my sister's door before pushing it open. She's frantically bouncing and rocking, attempting to calm, but instead, agitating.

"Trouble?" I ask.

< 156 >

"She's fed, she's changed, she's burped. I don't know how to make her happy." Gray crescents underscore her eyes and her hair looks like it hasn't been combed all day.

"You want me to take her for a drive? I hear that helps."

"Would you?" She unloads the baby into my arms, then, "No, I should come too."

"You don't have to." I cuddle Allison to my chest, happy to have a companion even if it's a tiny one who can't speak.

"I'm the food supply."

Five minutes later we're backing out of the driveway with mother and child ensconced in the back seat. It takes less than three minutes for Allison to grow quiet in her car seat.

"You know what I think is really wrong with the world?" Chloe asks, her disembodied voice floating from behind my head. "If you put on make-up that's SPF 15 and sun-screen that's SPF 15, that should count as 30 SPF, but it doesn't work that way and that just sucks."

"Why don't you close your eyes for a little while?"

By the time we reach the highway she, too, has sunk into slumber. Forty minutes later I take an unmarked left turn on to a two-lane bumpy road. The only illumination comes from my headlights. We are way, way out in the country. I'm startled when a massive shape rises up from the side of the road. An owl sweeps low, almost brushing the hood of the car. Something's wiggling in its talons – a mouse, I guess. Cool. I've never seen an owl outside of a zoo in my life. I certainly didn't know they were zooming around the Texas panhandle.

After about ten minutes, shadowy structures appear on the flat horizon. I slow down to five mph as I creep into Owensville. There's not a light on anywhere – not a porch light, not a street light. There are only a couple of streets laid out in a tic-tac-toe grid. They were smoothly paved

< 157 >

once but now they're pocked by deep potholes. Dilapidated wood-framed houses are circled by falling-down fences. Every structure leans toward the east, pressed by years of wind. The skeleton of a gas station marks the end of one street. Marking the end of the other is a long building with a faded sign propped against a splintery wall. My headlights illuminate the sign – Owensville Dance Studio. The school building dominates from the center position, proud and solid, the only thing out here that was built to last. I pull up in front of the steps of the school and turn off the car.

I didn't come out here planning to go walking around inside an old abandoned school in the middle of the night. It was just a place to drive to, that's all. But I'm here, so why not? I don't anticipate finding anything of value. And I can't stay in there for long because Chloe and Allison are asleep out here. Just a quick walk-through should satisfy.

Grabbing the flashlight from the glove compartment, I get out of the car. The wind whistles through the empty streets and sweeps the clouds across the dark sky. The moon hovers above the edge of the plain, creating odd shadows from ramshackle walls. I climb the steps to the school entrance. The front door is locked but right next to it, in the space where a window should be, there's a gaping thigh-high hole. I swing my leg over the sill and I'm in.

I cast my light to the high ceiling of the foyer and then back down to the floor. The windows have been gone for so long that the fine grit of the Great Plains has whipped in and through, creating foot-high drifts in corners and against walls. Newspapers and tumbleweeds are buried in the dirt. Somewhere nearby a cricket chirps. I detest crickets. They jump.

Right in front of me is a glass-fronted room that's

< 158 >

dominated by a long counter. Behind the counter are cubbies for mail and messages – obviously, the office. Other than that, I'm offered four choices – two hallways and two staircases. The hallways are of identical proportion and, because of the time constraint I don't dither, but slide quickly into the hallway on the right, stopping to scan the first room I come to. No furniture, no fixtures, just a big empty square with a chalkboard and busted windows. The second room's the same. I'm not going to find anything of interest on this floor. Turning back to the front of the building I take the set of stairs on the right.

The structure is rectangular and the floor plan is easily discerned – two mirrored halves on two levels. The two upstairs halls are connected mid-way by shorter crossing halls, each with a staircase coming from the side. I follow the cavernous hallway that opens before me, going straight to the back of the second level, crossing to the opposite hall, and heading back toward the front. I look into a few of the empty rooms on the way and, though I had no expectations, I'm still disappointed. There's nothing in here – not an old desk, not a pull-down map, not even a flagpole. I remind myself that it's not just about the stuff. It's about exploration; it's about going in and going around; it's about creeping through an abandoned building for no reason other than doing it.

When I'm near the top of the stairs, ready to get out of here, a sound from behind gives me pause. It's a clicking, scratching noise – *scritch, scritch*. Am I not alone in here? Have I been going through this closed-down school thinking it's empty when it's not? No, of course not. There's nobody here. And this noise doesn't sound like the movement of a person.

Scritch. Scritch. Closer this time.

< 159 >

I turn abruptly, shining my light toward the sound. And am so startled that I leap back.

A skunk. Followed by another, smaller skunk.

"Whoa, hey." I retreat further. They're only about five feet away. They're kind of cute, waddling along with their sparkling eyes and their white stripes. See, this is the kind of pill-induced logy detachment I'm talking about. I'm here, shining the bright beam of my flashlight into the eyes of approaching skunks, but I don't quite grasp the situation – not until the bigger skunk hisses at me, turns around, and lifts its tail.

"No!" I say, taking a gigantic step backward.

Only there's nothing behind me. I go tumbling.

< 160 >

A Pack in the Night

I return to consciousness to find my sister's face hovering over me. She holds a pink and white strip of some kind across her mouth and nose. My face is wet and my eyes are burning. Her eyes above her makeshift mask are tearing up, too.

"Is that a diaper?" I ask.

"I am so mad at you right now." Her voice is muffled.

"Why is my face wet?"

"I dumped water on you." She shakes a water bottle at me to prove it.

Disoriented, I'm sprawled at an angle with my head on a downward slant. Trying to lift my shoulder, I'm hit with a stab of pain in my left ankle.

"No, don't try to move yet. Your ankle's caught."

I lift my head. Sure enough, my foot's caught in the iron railing. I take further inventory. My shoulder and head are both throbbing.

"My head hurts." I press careful fingers to the back of my head and discover a tender lump the size of a robin's egg.

"Look at yourself. What were you thinking? You'll have to burn your clothes and shave your head." Stretching an arm under my shoulders, she attempts to help me shift the upper part of my body, but as she's reluctant to actually touch me and determined to keep the diaper pressed across her mouth and nose, her help isn't really that helpful.

< 161 >

As soon as I'm upright, I turn my leg, extricating my ankle, which seems swollen and sensitive but not intolerably painful. I shift around so that I'm sitting in a more reasonable position.

"I'm okay," I tell her. "I thought I was hurt, but I'm just bruised up."

"You're acrid. Just being near you is making me sick." She clambers further down the steps, emphasizing her point.

"I honest-to-God never saw it coming."

"It's what skunks do."

I stand. A stab of pain shoots up my leg.

"Yow!" I screech, coming off the ankle fast.

"I'm not touching you again. You'll have to get yourself out of here and to the car."

"Aren't doctor's supposed to be sympathetic?"

"I'm sure that someday I'll run into someone stupider than you, but right now I simply can't imagine it." With a huff, she marches down the stairs and out the door.

I hop down the stairs on my good leg, using the rail for support. Then I hop across the foyer, swing my legs over the sill, and hobble across the broad porch. Because these stairs offer no rail to use as a crutch, I sit on my butt and scoot down, holding my injured ankle up to keep from bumping it.

Chloe's got the car running, all the windows down, and the passenger door open. I one-leg it to the car, fall into the seat, and close the door.

"I just noticed something," she says.

"What?"

"Look out there." She points toward the falling-down house across the street.

I peer out the windshield. Small orange lights hover near and around the derelict structure. They appear and

< 162 >

reappear. Shadows shift. The orange lights are animal eyes. They're watching us.

"What is it? What are they?"

"Coyotes. Or wild dogs. A whole pack."

We walked before them. We were vulnerable. It never occurred to me to see if I was safe or if Chloe and Allison were safe. Predators watched me from right over there as I scooted down the steps.

"This has to stop." Chloe is as horrified as I am. "What if I hadn't been here?"

She's still got the diaper over her mouth and nose. She holds it there as we leave Owensville. She holds it there all the way to town and to the hospital, where she drops me at the emergency room to get my ankle X-rayed.

"What are you going to tell Mom?" I ask as I'm getting out of the car.

"The truth. You were driving Allison and me around because Allison was crying. You got out of the car for a few seconds, ran into a skunk, tried to get away, and fell and hurt your ankle."

"Thanks."

"You're going to owe me."

"I owe everybody."

She drives away in my car and I hop, shuffle, and limp toward the ER entrance, miserably resigned to running up another hospital bill.

< 163 >

Pretty Damned Good Luck

The emergency room charge is twelve hundred dollars. And that's with what they call the "employee's uninsured family members' discount." And they're also kind enough to allow me to make payments. Fifty dollars a month, another monthly disbursement for Mom to oversee. I wonder if Zachary will allow me a couple of more hours a week.

In addition, I'm stuck wearing this awkward and un-attractive boot – a blue and black molded contraption, held together by Velcro straps, and stabilizing the area from my toes to mid-calf. But at least it's my left ankle that's frac-tured so I'll be able to drive.

Having heard Chloe's version of what happened, Mom shows up at the hospital at around five to take me home. She exchanges greetings with the triage nurse, who tells her the best formula for removing skunk smell. I've been given at least five best methods, all delivered from behind filter masks. This has been a traumatic night.

"So, a skunk and a fractured ankle," Mom says. Not wanting skunk in her CRV, she brought my car. She slides into the driver's seat. All the windows are down and she's nabbed one of the filter masks from the emergency room.

"That pretty much says it all." I collapse into the passen-ger seat and fasten the seat belt.

< 164 >

"They give you Tylenol for the pain?"

"Yeah. It doesn't hurt all that bad – more like a deep ache."

"I believe a person makes her own luck," she says, "which makes me wonder why yours has been so bad lately."

"You think I brought this on myself?"

"Didn't you?"

Luck is contextual. I had a heart attack and could have died, but I didn't. I fell and cracked a small bone in my ankle when I could have broken my neck. I could have been bitten by a rattler or devoured by coyotes, but neither happened. If you ask me, my luck's been pretty damn good. When we get home Mom gives me a bucket of some kind of solution she's made – hydrogen peroxide, baking soda, and Dawn detergent – and instructs me to douse myself in it, leave it on for five minutes, then rinse it off.

"Keep doing it until you can't smell yourself anymore."

"I can't smell myself now," I tell her. "My sense of smell has been destroyed."

I clunk upstairs to follow her instructions.

"I could smell you as soon as you turned on to the street," Chloe calls as I pass her bedroom. I stop and peek in. Sitting on her bed and nestled into a bank of pillows, her feet are straight out in front of her and her toes are separated by wedges of cotton. Her heels are smooth and her toenails are pearly pink. Propped in her baby carrier next to Chloe, Allison is alert and happy. She, too, has pearly pink toenails.

"I'm glad you're finally doing something about your ratty feet," I say.

My clothes go in a closed trash bag that I'll put in the outside garbage. It takes the whole bucket of Mom's solution and seven one-legged showers before I feel like myself

< 165 >

again. I put on fresh clothes, adjust the hideous boot, and carry last night's jeans and T-shirt out to the trash container in the garage. Then I limp back inside and plant myself, ankle elevated, on the couch with the television control within reach. In addition to the hurt ankle, the bump on my head is tender and my shoulder is bruised. I don't intend to move all day.

It's funny how a single little baby can change the atmosphere of an entire house. Baby blankets, changing pads, tiny clothes, stacks of diapers – all these things have become fixtures in our living room. A bassinet is next to the arm of the couch and an ungainly stroller takes up space by the back door.

I wonder if Mom feels crowded. She's been alone in the house for the last three years and now, when she expected to have permanent peace, her two adult daughters and a baby have taken over. She walks through the living room, ready for work, at six-thirty.

"Are you resentful that your empty nest is no longer empty?" I ask.

"You need to keep off that ankle for a few days, so call Zachary and tell him you can't come in – but don't call him before nine." Typically, she ignores my question. Mom believes in dealing with what's in front of her, not what-might-have-beens. With a "talk to ya later" she's out the door.

It takes me five minutes to flick through every channel and find nothing to hold my interest. It takes me another five to realize that, relying on the busted ankle to keep me grounded, Mom won't be calling to check on me every few minutes. And, with the excuse of an injury to keep me from work, I have an unexpected free day.

Geraldine will show up at the mall claiming that we're friends and it's embarrassing to think that Karen and

< 166 >

Zachary will meet her and associate her with me. Also, it's only a matter of time before Geraldine comes here, to the house. It'll be best if I find her before she finds me.

Before I can go anywhere I've got to decontaminate my beloved car. The ingredients of Mom's formula are still out on the cabinet and I figure, hey, if it worked on me, it'll work on my car. So I mix the detergent, baking soda, and hydrogen peroxide in the same bucket I used earlier, limp out to the driveway, and start scrubbing the upholstery of the passenger seat. Scrub, rinse, scrub, rinse, scrub, rinse. When I'm finished I leave the doors standing open in the hope that it'll dry faster.

Chloe comes out on the driveway carrying Allison in a front-riding halter.

"You think that'll take care of it?" she asks, waving at someone across the street. Following her gaze, I see Jerry in the shadow of his garage, probably working on one of his birdhouses.

"What do you think? I still can't smell anything."

"You going somewhere?" She sniffs the air and makes a face.

"I've got errands."

Out on the street a silver Mercedes pulls up behind Chloe's VW. Henry Kearney gets out of the sedan and heads toward us. Wearing his regular khakis and golf shirt, he sends contradictory messages – his stride is firm and determined while his shoulders are hunched defensively; his brow is furrowed, but his lips are turned upward in a friendly smile.

"See?" Her hiss is furtive. "He keeps showing up here. I never know what to say to him."

"Girls! How wonderful to see you both. And Allison, pretty in pink." He opens his arms like he wants to take the

< 167 >

three of us in a big hug. "What a beautiful day the Lord has made! Chloe, I was hoping I could treat you and Allison to an early lunch – or brunch, if that's what you prefer to call it. Olivia, what in the world did you do to your foot?"

"I can't," Chloe tells him. "Allison and I have a doctor's appointment. We're getting ready to go right now."

She turns and hurries through the gate, leaving him standing there. I don't know what to think. How is it that she doesn't know how to decline an invitation without being rude? And what is it about him that sends her scurrying? I clearly don't understand what's going on between my sister and her father. Did they have some sort of disagreement during the time she stayed with him?

Thwarted, Henry remains there, unmoving and looking after her for half a minute. Then he turns toward me.

"Did you talk to her like you promised? Did you tell her to give me a chance to be her father?"

Did I talk to her? I'm pretty sure I did, but I can't remember the exact words.

"Sure," I say, "just like you asked. But she's her own person. She's not going to fall in line just because we had a conversation."

"I blame your mother. If it hadn't been for her I would've been part of Chloe's life all these years. But she kept Chloe from me. She kept me from my only child."

He pivots and marches back toward his car.

"Can I ask you something?" I call after him. "Don't you have a practice in Aimes? Why aren't you back there doing dermatologist things?"

"I took time off to be a father," he says over his shoulder.

I go in the house to find Chloe poised just to the side of the front window, peering out.

"He's just sitting out there," she says as I hobble up

< 168 >

beside her. "I guess now I have to go on out, load Allison in the car, and pretend to go to the doctor."

"Looks like it."

Why doesn't she just be nice to the guy? She was the one who contacted him – it just seems wrong that now she seems to want no part of him. If my father were to discover my existence and show an interest, I'd be open to getting to know him, wouldn't I?

She gathers her purse, keys, and baby supply bag and, with Allison still in the halter, leaves the house through the front door. I remain at the window.

As soon as Chloe approaches her car, Henry gets out of his and circles his hood. Ignoring him, she opens the passenger door of her VW and leans in to fasten Allison into the car seat. When she straightens he stands before her, palms open in supplication. He seems to be pleading with her. She tries to shift around him, but he steps to the side, too, blocking her way. When she moves to the other side, he once again mirrors her movement.

His open hands which had a second ago appeared benign and needy, take on a sinister aspect as he lifts them and takes a firm grasp on her upper arms.

And I'm out the door.

"Hey, you two," I call in a cheerful voice as I clumsily manage the three steps with my cumbersome boot. Henry releases her arms and retreats as I ask, "What's up? Chloe, you better get a move-on if you're going to make your appointment."

He returns to his car and drives away.

"What was that about?" I ask.

"He wanted to drive us to the doctor." Biting her lower lip, she keeps her eye on Henry's car as he turns from the block. "He's just really intense."

< 169 >

Across the street Jerry has stepped out of his garage and is looking in our direction. He's cradling one of his bird-houses in his arms like it's a baby. I give him a wave, signaling that everything's fine. He turns and goes back in.

< 170 >

Beneath the Matchbox Collection

Though I've made it my practice to pick a Bible passage randomly, if I divide the pages at the front or back there's no doubt as to where I'm going to end up. This morning I'm not in the mood for all the scary rambling of Isaiah or the ambiguity of the parables, so I stick my finger in toward the beginning, where the lessons are easily discernible. And sure enough, Genesis 29:22 – *Laban gathered all the men of the place and made a feast* – is a small verse right in the middle of the story about how Jacob worked for seven years to win Rachel's hand, but was tricked into marrying Rachel's myopic sister, Leah, instead. This verse is typical of the way the Biblical narrative so often implies rather than clearly states. At first glance, the sentence is insignificant – but in fact, the insinuation is highly relevant: Laban was able to fool Jacob into marrying the wrong sister by getting Jacob drunk.

What should I take from this? Considering my recent history, it would be easy to restate lessons learned about loss brought on by addiction. But I've been instructed to apply these spiritual messages to my life as it is today, to apply the points going forward, not backward. So I'll just be alert for people trying to manipulate me through schemes, which, come to think of it, is always a good thing to be alert about.

And now on with my day.

< 171 >

The Geraldine situation is bothersome, and I'd do anything to get out of paying her, but at this point I don't see any choice. If I want her out of my life it's going to cost me. I go to the bank and take out six hundred and fifty dollars.

It makes the most sense to begin my search in the last place I knew her to be. But there are only a few cars in the mall parking lot this early in the day, and none of them is Geraldine's green Toyota. I circle the whole mall, but no Geraldine.

Here's an inexplicable fact: drop a using addict in any town in the country and within a day that addict will have fallen in with a group possessed by a similar dependency. Caprock might not be a crowded metropolis, but it's a microcosm of one, and, just like any city, it has a seedy element, a number of rough people who float through the shadows of the north side where a few disreputable bars deal contraband from their back doors. The Geraldine I used to know would never have hung with the spooks that populate the Boulevard, but the woman I saw last night would fit right in. I turn my car to the highway and head toward the loser side of town.

There are several cheap hotels on the Boulevard and Geraldine's car is in front of a room at the third pitted parking lot I drive through. See, she lied about not having money for a place to stay. Here's another thing I know: addicts lie. I pull up beside her Toyota, clamber out and, dragging the hefty boot, give three firm taps on the door. She answers wearing the same clothes she had on last night. I didn't think it was possible for her to look more of a mess, but she does – hair all over the place, mascara smeared beneath her eyes. Her purse strap hangs on her shoulder and the room key is in her hand.

"Good morning, Sunshine," I say.

< 172 >

"You left me there, you bitch." She glances at my boot but doesn't ask what happened.

"But I'm here now. On your way out?"

"Coming to find you."

"Here." I hold out the money. She counts it.

"This is only six hundred and fifty dollars."

"I told you – Vernon gets his share."

"Thirteen hundred, that's what you owe."

"Take it or leave it. I borrowed from both of you and I'm paying both of you back."

Her eyes cut to the left as she thinks about her alternatives.

"The highway's that way," I tell her, pointing south. "To the right is California. Left, Oklahoma and beyond."

I return to my car and reverse out of there. When I look in my rearview mirror she's still standing in the doorway, cash in hand. She better put the bills away and get out of here. This is not a good neighborhood.

The money gone from my account makes me feel like I'm missing part of myself. My breath is short and my sinuses are swelling because I'm holding back tears. I won't feel whole again until I replace it. If that Tiffany lamp out at Meskar's is in good shape it's worth more than what I just gave away. I've got the time and my gear is in the trunk.

No jumping over the fence from the roof of the car today. With the heavy blanket across my back, I wriggle under the barbed wire. The cows must be going about their business elsewhere because they're not in sight. I've noticed people wearing boots like the one I'm wearing now and it never occurred to me that getting around with one of these things brings on a whole set of issues. Like the sole of the shoe on my right foot is a different height than the boot, which means I rock with every step I take, which gets my hips and back involved. And the boot is hard. There's no

< 173 >

cushion, just dense inflexible plastic. Also, it's heavy, which means it's not long before my quads and calves are tensing in preparation for every step. By the time I'm halfway to the house I ache all over.

Never an easy task, climbing the ladder and transferring to the deck is a dangerous exertion. But finally, scaring myself only once, I clump across the deck to the door. And once again I'm in the Meskar Mansion.

The portrait of Eubert Meskar greets me like an old friend. Exhausted and sore, I drag the annoying boot around the desk, flop into the chair, and elevate my swollen ankle. After a few minutes of massaging my leg and catching my breath, I open the top center drawer and find boring office supplies – paper clips, a stapler, scissors, rubber bands. The bottom drawers are deep and hold racked folders, which are alphabetized and seem to contain various receipts and records, some dated from as far back as the nineteen-thirties.

I open the right-hand middle drawer and – oh, for goodness sake – it holds a collection of matchbox cars. I stick my hand in and pluck up a few of the small toys. From the fifties or sixties is my guess. There are probably fifty of them. I don't think they're worth a lot. But really, how did they come to be here, in a businessman's desk? Did he play with them when he got bored? How long did it take him to assemble this collection? Was he sentimental about them?

Beneath the cars, fitted so tightly into the bottom of the drawer that I almost miss it, is an A4 manila envelope. I push the cars to the side and dig at the corners of the envelope with my fingernails to get it out of there. It was probably glued closed at one point, but the glue is old and the flap is free. I extract a couple of sheets of paper. The heading of the top sheet reads "Last Wishes of Eubert Bartholomew Meskar."

< 174 >

I slip the papers back into the envelope and insert the envelope into the depths of my backpack. Then, as an afterthought, I shovel all the cars in as well. I step-thump downstairs.

Tucked into a shadowy corner of the front room, the lamp is impressive. About five feet tall, the iron stand is solid with an ornate vine circling the broad round base and reaching halfway up the post. The graceful bell-shaped shade follows an intricate blossom and dragonfly motif – and, most important of all, every tiny pane is intact. The colors are dulled by years of neglect, but I feel good about its condition. My limited research has revealed a dynamic market so full of imitations from the same period – late eighteen, early nineteen hundreds – that identifying this as an original Tiffany would be costly and likely impossible. On the other hand, the reproductions sell for almost as much, so I'm going to post it as "mint" and "unauthenticated."

The cord and plug are yellowed and cracked, though, and I can't sell it as mint if doesn't work, so rewiring is my new priority.

I wrap the cord around the stand and, grasping the pole firmly, lift it. It's heavy.

Twenty minutes later I'm wondering if I have the strength to make it back to the car. I've only come halfway and my arms are straining and my pounding heart feels too large for my chest. The sun is giving me a headache and the hot wind is drying me out. I wish I'd brought my water bottle with me instead of tossing it so carelessly toward the passenger seat. Also, in addition to my physical misery, I'm having one of those surreal moments where I'm viewing myself from a distance. And what I see is incongruent. Who'd have thought that a lamp so delicate would be so

< 175 >

heavy? And who is this limping fool lugging this unexpect-edly substantial item across the middle of nowhere?

Seriously, what am I doing? This period after rehab is supposed to be a growing time, a time when I become comfortable with who I am without cocaine. Yet look at me, looting a state-owned house, tripping around skunk-infested buildings in the middle of the night. Stealing mixing bowls, for God's sake. The plan was to evolve into a better version of myself, but there doesn't seem to be a better version, only a clean one. So be it. I may not be good, but I'm interesting.

And that's when my phone rings. It's Mom.

"Where are you?" Her voice is angry and impatient.

"Out for a walk."

"You're supposed to be sitting on the couch with your foot elevated. Go straight home right now." She disconnects.

And my foot-dragging turns into stomping. I hate this. I hate the fact that my mother has the right to talk to me like I'm a misbehaving seven-year-old. It's not until I'm gently manipulating the lamp through the barbed wire that I realize that stomping on a broken ankle isn't a good idea. Now not only do I feel shaky and tender all over, but my ankle, which up to this point has only been mildly sore, is throbbing. I crawl under the fence, catching the boot twice – once on a clump of dirt, and again on the wire. In order to get my new acquisition in the trunk I'm going to have to disassemble it. I twist the pole from the base, remove the wing nut at the top, and tuck an old towel around the shade to protect it from breakage. Then, as instructed by my mother, I go straight home.

As soon as I'm through the back door I grab my laptop from the kitchen table, stagger to the couch, and prop my foot on the coffee table. Here's my journal entry for the day:

< 176 >

An old friend stopped by the store last night. I'm not supposed to talk to ex-cohorts and I got rid of her as quickly as I could. But rather than tempt me to return to my out-of-control lifestyle, which I assume is the concern behind the rule, seeing her again made me ashamed of what I must have been just a few short months ago.

Am I ashamed? No, not really. It's more like I'm resigned to a then-and-now reality. But this fluffy blurb should appease a Caprock parole officer. In actuality, my feelings concerning Geraldine are ambivalent. Everything about her evoked memories – the slight slur to her speech, her narrow shoulders, the way she squints when she talks about money. She and I had good times. Seeing her made me miss the rush that made everything, especially me, wonderful. And at the same time it made me sad that there is no such thing as a balance. An addict is either climbing up or sliding down.

< 177 >

Two Mothers

I still smell faintly of skunk.

The will I found in Meskar's desk was signed and dated thirty years before he died, probably a year or two before he left the area. When he died four years ago, the will that left the Bandera home to a charitable trust made no mention of the panhandle property, and that's how it came to be in the hands of the state. But in this older document he willed the Caprock house and acreage to someone named Joyce Rittenhauer.

I look her up. She died last year, survived by a daughter, Penelope. Is there a possibility that Penelope was Meskar's daughter? No. She was born a couple of years after he moved away. But if Joyce Rittenhauer had come into possession of the property she probably would have left it to her daughter. But this didn't happen and so it doesn't mean a thing. Or does it? If Joyce left her possessions to her daughter that would include the Meskar Mansion, even if she wasn't aware that it belonged to her.

And now I'm curious. Where is Penelope now? What did she make of herself? What was in her mother's will? There's every chance she didn't leave one. For the most part, people in and around Caprock aren't wealthy and they have nothing to leave behind. If, toward the end of a life, there's any money, it goes to pay the costs of dying.

< 178 >

Chloe and Allison come in through the front door. Chloe heads toward the couch, flops down on the opposite corner from me, drops the diaper bag at her feet, and starts fiddling with the straps of the baby carrier that's hooked around her torso. Red-cheeked and damp at the temples, she brings the heat of the outdoors with her.

"Where've you guys been?"

"Transferring and getting registered. Nothing's ever simple. It's going to take the whole rest of the summer to get this done." She extricates Allison from the halter with one hand while, with the other, she grabs the changing pad from the coffee table and spreads it on the couch. "Fill out this form, fill out that form, make this payment before that payment, you can't do this until you do that, don't stand in this line until you've stood in that one."

"Yeah."

Gently flopping Allison down and unsnapping the inseam of the tiny jammies, she strips off the diaper. Allison kicks her legs and gazes at her mother, taking every action seriously.

"Can I show you something?" Chloe asks.

"Sure."

Keeping a hand firmly on her diaperless baby's round tummy, she reaches into the diaper bag, lifts out a folded paper rectangle, and holds it toward me. I accept and unfold it. It's a check made out to her for fifteen thousand dollars.

"Wow." I peer at the signature. "Graham Vickles? Allison's father?"

"Should I keep it? Should I tell Mom? What would she do if she were me? What would you do?"

What I'd do is easy. I'd never tell Mom. I'd stick the money in the bank and let the thought of it give me

< 179 >

comfort when I was scared, encouragement when I was lonely, inspiration when I was despondent. I'd make up songs about it. I'd spend hours thinking up uses for it. Hey, there's a hobby – fantasizing about having money.

She efficiently wraps and tapes Allison's diaper and redoes the snaps. Nestling into the cushions, she lifts up her shirt, pushes her soft bra over her boob, and pokes her nipple into Allison's mouth. Allison wiggles all over in ecstasy, then settles. A peculiar expression crosses Chloe's face – pain and pleasure. Her lips part in a sigh.

"What are you feeling? What's making you look that way?"

"It's like nothing I've ever felt before," she says. "First I'm so full of milk that it hurts, then there's a release as the milk starts to flow and it feels so good it's practically orgasmic. Seriously, I feel it all the way to my uterus."

"Wow."

"I guess it kind of depends on what it means." Oh, she's back to the check. "Guilt, concern, a buy-off. Do you think that's what it is – hush money?"

"Would that keep you from accepting it?"

"Pretty sure, yeah. I hate it when people try to manipulate me. And trying to control what I say or do with money, well that's reprehensible. Plus, he should know he can trust me. I'd never knock on his door making threats or demands." She's more like Mom than I realized.

"Maybe he's got a sense of responsibility and he's doing the best he can."

She grows silent and after a minute or two I turn on the television. I'm pretty hungry and am considering the satisfaction to be found in a sandwich. Chloe lifts Allison to her shoulder, rubbing the baby's back until a nice milky burp rises and leaks spit-up all over Chloe's T-shirt. Chloe

< 180 >

places groggy Allison in the bassinet and settles back into the cushions. Within seconds they're both asleep.

I pull the blanket from the back of the couch and toss it over her.

And my eyes drift closed, too.

Hours later Mom shakes my shoulder. She's changed out of her work clothes and into jeans and a flowery blouse. The blanket's draped over me, and Chloe and Allison are gone.

"Oh," I say.

"I'm on my way to the attorney's. About that lawsuit."

"Can I come?" I straighten, struggling to wake up.

"Why?" She sniffs, testing the air around me. "You're still smelly."

"I'll stay downwind." I pop off the couch. I feel really good, almost chemically enhanced good. I needed the sleep.

"Comb your hair first."

I clumsily rush upstairs to brush my hair and wash my face. Five minutes later we're in the car on the way to Mom's lawyer's office. Ravenous, I stuff an open-faced bread and cheese sandwich at my mouth. The envelope containing notification of the lawsuit is a blight on the dashboard.

"This guy charges one-fifty for half an hour," she says.

"What if you only need fifteen minutes? If you take up a single minute do you only get charged five dollars?"

"Don't be a smarty-mouth."

It turns out the lawyer is Joe Esposito. We graduated the same year, took three years of Latin together. I remember him as being darkly good-looking, smart, with a sense of fun. He meets us at the receptionist's desk, invites us back. His office is opulent – old-fashioned landscapes, heavy furniture, a Turkish carpet on the floor – not the setting I would have pictured him in.

< 181 >

"Olivia, it's good to see you. What happened to your foot?" His measured tone indicates that he's heard all about my addictive affair with Whitey, and he's not surprised to see me with an injured appendage.

"Nothing serious. You look good."

Mom, seated and waiting, has no patience with niceties. She shifts in the deep cushion of the leather chair and Joe turns his attention her way.

"How can I help?"

She hands him the notification of the lawsuit, which he reads. When finished, he returns the paper to its envelope and pushes the call button on his desk. A few seconds later a towering woman with a helmet of brassy hair enters. He hands her the envelope and asks her to scan its contents. Then he addresses Mom.

"Tell me your version."

Mom covers the whole thing. Now and then Joe nods sympathetically. When she's finished Mom wraps her arms around her chest, an uncharacteristically defensive gesture.

"How would this look from Chloe's point of view?" he asks, his expression deliberately impassive. "Would she say you did what they're claiming you did?"

"I saw my daughter making a mistake and I spoke up. I did what a mother does."

Joe's assistant returns, places the envelope on the corner of the desk, and departs.

"Okay, here's what I'm going to suggest. I'll contact their lawyer on your behalf, see what's what, and get back to you."

"What does 'see what's what' mean?"

"This is an emotional issue. People are hurt. And when people are hurt their first instinct is to strike out. I'll talk to

< 182 >

him, he'll talk to me, I'll get a picture of what we're dealing with. Then we'll discuss our next step."

"Okay," she says, but I can tell she's not satisfied. He hands her the envelope and, though she's obviously reluctant, she accepts it. She wanted to walk out of here with the issue resolved. She puts her purse strap over her shoulder, preparing to leave.

I came with my own agenda.

"I have a quick question," I say. "I'm doing research for an article – can I run something by you?"

Mom releases her purse and looks at me with a mixture of relief and exasperation. She's happy I'm showing an interest in writing, but irritated that I've horned in on her meeting. Joe lifts his chin attentively and makes a small "let's have it" motion with his fingers.

"If someone leaves a property to someone in a will, only the will is tucked away and the beneficiary is unaware – and then the beneficiary dies leaving his or her possessions to their child, and then the original will is discovered, does the survivor inherit what the beneficiary never even knew was theirs in the first place?"

"The will's signed, dated, witnessed? Not superseded by a later will?"

"There is a later will, but it makes no reference to the property mentioned in the first will."

"Then yes, the first will would be valid."

I thank him and we take our leave. On the way home both of us are quiet, tiptoeing tentatively through our own thoughts.

< 183 >

Baseless Snob

Jane's wearing a gray turtleneck. While the color suits her, her neck is too short for the high collar, which makes her look jowly. Why am I so critical of her appearance? No one else receives such harsh scrutiny from me – so why does she?

"I saw Joe Esposito yesterday," I tell her. "Remember him?"

"He's married with kids now."

"Isn't everybody?"

"Is that resentment in your tone?"

If she hears resentment it's because that's what she wants to hear. Smug and self-absorbed, she can't imagine that anyone would want a life different than the one she's constructed for herself. If I do feel resentment, and I'm not saying I do, it's directed inward. The life I had was the life I wanted and through weakness and stupidity, I lost it. But okay, I'll manufacture some malaise if it'll kill the hour.

"I think I'm more frustrated than resentful," I tell her. "There's nothing going on in this town. What do adults in Caprock do when they're not walking down the aisle, procreating, or adoring their progeny?" I'm being snide but she doesn't seem to catch it.

"There's loads of stuff for singles to do." Her eyes light up. She's thrilled that I'm showing signs of conformity.

< 184 >

"Softball at the sports complex nearly every night. I'm pretty sure the mall has a team. And every church in town has some kind of singles' class."

Softball and church. Oh boy.

When she starts going on about a barbecue her church's women's group is sponsoring for their singles' class, I let my mind wander. It's going to cost ninety dollars to get the lamp re-wired. It's an exorbitant amount, but there's only one electrical repair shop in town, so I had no choice. I dropped it off this morning and I can pick it up tomorrow.

Here's what I learned when I looked into Joyce Rittenhauer's daughter, Penelope, called Penny: She married at twenty, had two kids, got divorced, and works as a dental hygienist; she's twenty-eight and her children are seven and five. I've got her address. The will waits in the passenger seat of my car.

"Olivia?"

"I'm sorry. My mind wandered. What did you say?"

"I was asking about your journal. I understand you're sharing it with Ariana Smoot."

It takes me a second to place the name. Smoot. My parole officer.

"Not willingly. A journal should be private."

"I agree, and that's why I never asked to see it. But if she has access to it, I should have access to it, too. I'm your counselor. She's just a monitor."

"You shouldn't be discussing me with her."

"We consult. We're your team."

"My team." I've never been a team player. Also, the people on my team should be people I've chosen, not people who are assigned. Unable to suppress my dismay, I say, "Please tell me my time's up."

"We've got five minutes."

< 185 >

She spends the rest of the time talking about hobbies I could take up. The Caprock Community Center is starting a class on shoe design she thinks I'd enjoy.

When Penny Rittenhauer was married she took her husband's last name, Brandt. But when she got divorced she went back to her maiden name. And she changed the kids' last names, too, which leads me to the unsubstantiated conclusion that there must have been such bad feelings between her and her ex that she didn't even want her kids to carry his name.

As soon as Jane sets me free I aim my car toward the south side of town, which is where Penny lives. The houses in her neighborhood are three-bedroom, one-and-a-half baths, with low ceilings. Built in the early sixties, they provided affordable and comfortable housing for the blue collar workers of a flourishing economy. These days the homes are in varying condition – some have been updated and others have been left to fall over; some have been added on to until they fill every foot of their lots, and some are still tiny square structures with car ports and shingle siding; some have yards of dirt and weeds while others have watering systems and healthy green lawns. It's an oddly disparate area.

Penny's house falls in between. An attempt has been made to maintain it. The trim's been painted in the last couple of years, the roof is in good shape, and the fence around the backyard looks new. But keeping a healthy lawn is one of the biggest challenges for homeowners in this part of the world, and somebody's given up on this one; it's mainly composed of dandelions. The single elm looks scrawny and dry. And weeds poke through the cracks in the driveway.

I park on the street. People clear out of here during the

< 186 >

day. Other than the wind pushing at tree branches, there's no activity in any direction. I reach for the envelope and get out of the car. I'm pretty sure no one's home. Penny works and, as it's summer, her kids'll be in some kind of day care program. As expected, no one answers the bell. I stick the will in the side of the door. Then I remove it. I put it in the mailbox that's mounted beside the door. Then I take it out again.

Hugging the envelope to my chest, limping off the small porch, I shuffle along the driveway around to the back of the house, glancing through the side windows as I pass. The gate to the backyard opens with an unexpectedly loud *breek!*

A slab of cement forms a simple patio off a set of sliding doors. The yard is weeds and dirt. There's no equipment or any sign that anybody ever comes back here. I approach the door and give a yank and a jiggle. It's locked. I cup my hands against the glass and peer into the living room. A couch and a chair face a television cabinet. Off to the left is the kitchen. A box of cereal rests on the kitchen table. It's all very ordinary.

This is the hottest time of day and the sun is beating down on this barren backyard. The fence blocks the breeze. There's nothing out here to sit on and so I perch on the edge of the uncomfortable porch, sticking my booted appendage straight in front of me, and lighting a cigarette. Why am I here at this woman's house peeking through her windows? If the back door hadn't been locked would I have gone in? Yes, I believe I would have. I have questions. Where does a dental hygienist buy her clothes? What does she read? What's in her refrigerator?

I came intending to leave the will. It'd be a nice surprise for her. I imagine her finding it in her mailbox. "What's

< 187 >

this?" she'd ask. She'd open it, realize what she held in her hand, squeal in excitement, and gather her kids in for happy hugs. Then she'd get a lawyer to help her jump through the legal hoops, and in a matter of weeks she'd own the Meskar Mansion and all the land surrounding it.

Then she'd sell. Why wouldn't she? It's not like she'd want to live out there among the cattle and mesquite. And she's not going to get sentimental about a fusty old house, not when she could buy a nice house in a better part of town and have some money to set aside for her kids' educations.

I can't leave the will. I'll get it to her eventually, but not yet. Once again I find myself crossing the line between doing what's right and doing what I want. It was one thing to take things from there when I thought it belonged to the state, but now I'm intentionally taking items that belong to someone who, from the look of things, could use the money. I have, through my excursions, come to think of the house as mine, which it plainly isn't. But I've grown fond of it, even come to identify with it – abandoned, alone, unloved. I'm not any of those things, not really, but sometimes I feel like I am.

Another issue comes to mind as the sun heats my shoulders and the smoke fills my lungs. Jane accused me of harboring resentment, but what I really felt, what I've always felt, was that I was better. I view myself as smarter, more talented, unique, non-traditional. But these are shallow comparatives; none of them was a bit of help when I stumbled. So what the hell do I have to feel superior about? Taking on humility, accepting it, is part of rehab, yet I'm pretty sure I conveyed my disdain toward the values and lifestyle that Jane obviously holds dear. No wonder she doesn't like me. I'm a baseless snob, a detractor. I was nicer when I was on cocaine.

< 188 >

I stub my cigarette into the dirt and, not wanting to leave evidence of my presence, hold on to the butt. When I get to the street I drop it in the gutter. I get back in the car, lock the envelope in the glove compartment, and drive home, where I spend a productive hour researching Matchbox cars.

The drawer contained more cars than I originally estimated – I'd thought between fifty and sixty, but there are seventy-three. The Matchbox collectors' website lists a range of prices – five to two hundred, depending on the rarity. To price and sell them individually would be a tedious process and, though there's the possibility that the collection contains one or two of the more valuable cars, it's a risk I'm willing to take. I list the whole set for three-fifty.

All my broken ankle got me was one day off work. I told Zachary I could work from four to closing, which means I'm driving out of the driveway as Mom's driving in. I wave at her and she sends me a glare that lets me know she knows I haven't been where I was supposed to be.

"Hey, Hop-along," Zachary says as I limp in. "How's the ankle?" Slumped over his worktable, his eyes are huge behind the magnifying lenses he wears when he's creating.

"You coming over tonight?" I ask after I've stuffed my purse in the safe in the back room.

"Sure."

"I'll have to elevate my ankle, but other than that, it's fine." It'll be no problem to prop my foot up on another chair.

"That boot's sure ugly."

"Can't argue with that. Karen already gone home?"

"She's asking for the first week of August off."

"She's got a family. She needs time off every once in a while."

< 189 >

"Yeah. But still."

"Can I ask you something? Caprock has got to be the most narrow-minded conventional place in the whole country." I'm referring to Jane's supposition that everyone's goal is to couple-up and make babies. "Why do you live here? How have you kept from going crazy?"

"I like it here. In summer the dry heat feels good to my bones, and at night the breeze is clean and fresh and I just can't imagine anywhere else being as comfortable. Last winter we had a blizzard that brought the whole area to a standstill. The wind swept up snowdrifts as high as my roof. I hunkered down in front of the TV and didn't get dressed for a week." He squints toward the opposite wall of the store, seeing some imaginary High Plains snowscape; and for a second he looks like what he pretends to be – a contemplative rough-skinned cowboy, rather than what he is – a gay designer of exquisite jewelry.

"That's it? Because of extreme weather?" I ask, disbelieving. "How can that be? You've traveled, you've seen what's out in the world. How can you live in a place that's so inert? How can you tolerate a place that won't tolerate you?" The majority of people here hang on to their prejudices. In the matter of social mores, Caprock is far from enlightened. I've witnessed people come into the store and walk out when they see what he is. I've heard other mall employees call him an old fag. It's ugly stuff.

"There's something wrong everywhere you go," he says. "Here, things don't move too fast. I like my house. And I don't handle change well, which is something you know about me." He gathers his leather satchel and, with a "See you later," walks out into the mall and heads toward the exit.

It was egocentric of me to assume that he feels the same

< 190 >

way about Caprock that I do. But he's right about not liking change. He hasn't changed his style of dress or clothes since he was eighteen. I've seen pictures. Also, he didn't say, but I suspect, that he wouldn't thrive without his best and only friend, my mom. Though sex isn't on the table, the two of them are as comfortable as an old married couple, which also comes under the heading of not liking change.

During my five hours on the clock I write a journal entry – three hundred words – in which I manage to relate absolutely nothing.

And I scroll through some of the abandoned Texas buildings websites. Old Route 66 offers several possibilities. Several boarded-up cafes look interesting (but are probably snake-infested). In one picture an empty strip mall is completely covered by tumbleweeds. There's a church in Camille, a tiny town fifty-five miles west and a little north of I-40. After the skunk incident I've decided that explorations at night aren't a good idea, but a church in daylight might be a fun walk-through.

Exactly six customers wander in. Bored and lonely, I'm pathetically glad to see them. I sell nothing. But Byroni Frain (zombie starlet) calls wanting Zachary to design her and her fiancé's wedding rings, so while no money has walked through the door, he'll soon have big bucks coming out of Hollywood.

Out in the mall Wally Roach and his partner walk by. He lifts his chin toward me, a dismissive gesture he probably practiced in front of the mirror, but they don't come in.

Also, of mild interest, a new fashion trend seems to be taking hold – middle-aged women wearing ankle-high mismatched colorful socks with Velcro-strapped hiking sandals. What are they thinking?

I'm glad when it's time to close up and clock out. The

< 191 >

mall employees flow toward the east exit, some walking together and talking, but most making the migration in a silent solitary stupor.

Geraldine's Toyota is parked next to mine in the parking lot. Vernon leans against its front fender, legs crossed at the ankle, arms crossed over his chest. Well, it's not like I haven't been halfway expecting it.

"Hey, Vernon." I'm not going to ask how he got the car back; that's probably one of those things I'm better off not knowing. A picture of Geraldine lying beat up in a ditch pops into my mind; I shut it down. Though I have my key in my hand, I don't click it. Wally's police car is parked in the next row, over a couple of cars. I lean against my own fender, facing Vernon, mirroring his posture.

"What'd you do to your foot?" He's not a big guy. In fact, he's a few inches shorter than I am. With even features, good teeth and shiny hair, he's attractive in a scruffy way.

"Fell down some stairs."

"I'm here for what you owe me." Some of my friends thought he was sexy – and I could understand that because when he's in a light-hearted mood he can be charming. Personally, I find him both menacing and fascinating. There's no telling when a new disposition will seize him, and there's no sense of a line he won't cross. I once saw him almost slice a guy's nose off because of a chess game. It took three men to pull him off. I wish I'd sent him the money instead of waiting and hoping he'd forget about it.

"Only half. I borrowed from both of you and I already gave the other half to Geraldine."

"I don't give a shit about whatever deal you cooked up with her. It was my money and I want it back." He slides two steps toward me so that our toes are almost touching. His eyes glitter maliciously. His stale warm breath goes

< 192 >

right into my face. I'd retreat but I'm trapped between him and my car. "Not some piddly-assed payment, not half. The whole amount."

He captures my right hand in both of his and lifts it to his chest, a deceptively affectionate gesture – deceptive in that he's captured my little finger and is bending it back, straining the joint. It hurts, but not as much as it might. I'm a scared sissy – wide-eyed and gasping. Tears flood as he keeps the pressure on. All it would take is a snap. Wally's over there, sitting in his car, watching. What does this look like to him? A man and woman, standing between two cars, close enough to kiss.

"The whole amount," Vernon tells me again, increasing the pressure. "Say it."

"The whole amount." I'll do what I have to do. My heart grieves.

He releases the finger, but continues to grasp my hand.

"I'll meet you right here," I say. "Tomorrow, one o'clock."

"Okay then." Holding my eyes, he lifts my hand to his lips and places a kiss in the palm; then he folds my fingers over the palm, as though protecting something precious. He replaces my hand at my side with exaggerated care and steps away; but then he gives a sudden lunge, the way bullies do when they want to make you cringe. I oblige by cringing. He emits a mean chuckle, turns to his car, gets in, and drives away.

< 193 >

Henry Goes Crazy

Wally's police car is framed in my rearview mirror as I drive home. I wonder what he thought of my encounter with Vernon.

In addition to Chloe's VW and Zachary's Cadillac, Henry Kearney's Mercedes is parked on the street in front of the house. Well good; Henry's in there having his say. Hopefully he'll find some peace about this whole situation. I bet Zachary's in histrionic heaven. I pull into the garage, enter the backyard through the side door, and look in through the glass of the kitchen door before I open it.

Zachary and Mom are on the couch in the living room. Straight-backed, they're so close to each other that their shoulders are touching – hardly relaxed couch-sitting. Also, ordinarily there'd be a couple of glasses of wine on the coffee table in front of them, but the glasses of red stand untouched on the counter in the kitchen.

Henry stands with his back to me. He's dressed in his usual khakis and collared shirt, and his hairless dome reflects the overhead light. I hear the low-pitched murmur of his voice but I can't make out what he's saying.

The couch is at a slant toward the back of the house and Mom sees me at the door. Her eyes get big and she gives an infinitesimal shake of her head, which is vexing because she knows I'm not good at reading silent signals. People

< 194 >

should use words. Beside her Zachary squints malevolently at Henry, which is out of character; his usual expression in an emotionally fraught situation is one of wicked glee.

"Hey, guys, what's going on?" I ask as I open the door and drag my weary booted foot inside.

"Olivia, come in and join the party." Henry's invitation is cheerful, though it's odd that he doesn't turn to greet me, but continues to face Mom and Zachary. When I limp around him, I see why. He's got a gun clasped close to his chest and pointed at them.

I'm really tired and my whole body aches from rocking around on this boot. Exhaustion, plus my meds, has brought on the familiar floating feeling, making this scene I've just limped into seem distant and unreal.

"Henry, what the hell." I take a few lopsided steps further into the room.

"Chloe's gone upstairs to get Allison and pack her things." He motions me toward the couch with little directional jerks of the gun. "Then they're coming home with me so we can spend some time together."

The man's fixated. I'm pretty sure Chloe's upstairs calling the cops. But, oh no; her pink phone is on the coffee table.

I hobble around to the back of the couch and hover behind Mom and Zachary.

"You've got something to say, Henry, so say it." The tremor in my voice surprises me. "You don't need to hold us at gunpoint to get us to listen."

"Sit down and be quiet."

I don't sit down but he doesn't seem to notice. After yesterday's scene by Chloe's car I figured he was volatile, but I didn't think he was insane. He doesn't look insane. He drives a nice car and he's a doctor. He's well-groomed and his features are even and attractive. Like Chloe pointed out,

< 195 >

he's intense, but until this he seemed reasonable. Even now, standing in front of us, he looks like a normal guy. His gaze is placid, his posture is relaxed, and his mouth curves into a friendly smile – all while he's pointing a gun at us. And now I've learned the lesson about how looks can be deceiving.

"Chloe! Time to go!" he bellows toward the stairs. Mom and Zachary both give startled jumps at his unexpected volume.

"Just a few more minutes," she calls back in a voice that's deliberately lacking anxiety.

The tiniest movement at the kitchen door catches my attention. Wally Roach's bodiless face appears on the other side of the glass, then fades away.

Mom tenses for a second.

"Honestly, Henry," she says. "You were married at the time. I did what I thought was best."

Wally's glittering eyes then appear at the side window. From that angle he'll be able to see the gun. Once again his face disappears.

"You kept her away from me for her whole life and now you're keeping her away from me again." I wonder how long this whining has been going on.

Wally returns to the back door. The handle turns and his hand reaches in as he slowly, slowly widens the gap between the door and its frame. I'm tense all over waiting for the door to squeak.

"You left town. You got on with your life," Mom says, holding his focus, speaking louder in an effort to cover any sound Wally might make.

"You want me to go check on Chloe?" I ask, helping to distract. Not waiting for a response, I move to the bottom of the stairs and holler, "Chloe? You okay?"

"I'll be right down!" she calls.

< 196 >

"Get back over there," Henry orders me.

"You were married," Mom says again. "It's not like we were in a committed relationship."

Wally's all the way in. He eases the door closed. Baton in hand, he tiptoes toward Henry. It's like watching a pale gorilla do ballet.

"She was the only child I ever had," Henry says. "All I want is to get to know my daughter."

"Of course you should get to know her." Mom's tone is reasonable, placating. "No one's stopping you."

Only a couple of feet behind Henry, Wally lifts the baton above his head.

"You're stopping me," Henry says. "You're keeping her—"

And Wally cracks the baton down on Henry's head. Henry's eyes roll back as he gracefully sways, then begins to sink. But as he goes down his gun hand knocks against the coffee table and …

Pop!

… I'm slammed into the wall behind me.

When Henry hits the floor Wally's partner charges through the back door, gun pointed as she scans all corners. She holsters her weapon, pulls out her phone, and reports, "Suspect down. Area secure."

Wally jumps on Henry's unconscious form and, as he cuffs him, shouts his rights at him.

"You have the right to remain silent! Anything you say at this time can be used against you in court. You have the right to an attorney… "

"Are you okay?" Chloe asks as she flies down the stairs. Disbelieving, hysterical, wild-eyed. "He shot at you?"

"Mom?" My voice sounds pitiful. My shoulder burns like it's on fire.

< 197 >

As one, Mom and Zachary turn toward me. Chloe takes the last three steps in one bound, coming to a stop a couple of feet in front of me.

"Oh no, Olivia," she says.

I look down at my shoulder. Blood is spreading across the ivory shell that I purchased two years ago at Neiman's and still haven't paid for.

"He shot me," I say, rationally pointing out, "but I simply can't afford another hospital bill."

< 198 >

Celebration

A gunshot wound to the shoulder costs roughly four times more than a broken ankle. Henry Kearney will ultimately be held responsible, but in order for that to happen I'm going to have to hire a lawyer and sue for it. Meanwhile, the bill for four-and-a-half thousand dollars is in my name.

By the time I'm signed out it's almost noon. I feel like I've been in the hospital for days instead of hours.

The sky is the bluest I've ever seen and the wind, which usually smells of the stockyards and carries the sting of fine grit, is pure and clean. It's a beautiful morning.

Mom is driving me home. I limp to her car and collapse into the passenger seat. She doesn't say a word as she steers from the parking lot. Nor does she speak as she drives. I've never seen her so lacking in animation. Stiff-shouldered and jittery from too much coffee, she's aged twenty years since yesterday. Though she's been with me most of the night, this is the first chance we've had to talk.

"Aren't you going to tell me I brought this on myself?" I'm joking. It's what she said last time she drove me home from the emergency room, though the notion of self-sabotage in this instant is ludicrous. But I'm hoping to tease her out of her dark mood.

It doesn't work. She stares ahead, gripping the wheel so hard her knuckles are white.

< 199 >

"It wasn't your fault," I tell her, taking her brooding as an indication that she's contemplating her part in this – namely, that she kept Chloe's existence from Henry Kearney.

"Of course not," she says. "It was yours."

"What?" My voice squeaks with indignation. "How is getting shot remotely my fault?"

"You made a target of yourself, standing behind the sofa like that instead of sitting down and being quiet. And you're the one who told Chloe to contact him. You're the one who suggested he might have something to offer."

"Strictly speaking, it was Zachary who brought it up first."

"But you encouraged her."

"Fine. Blame me." I rest my head back and close my eyes. My right arm is in a sling. The whole right side of my chest hurts every time I draw a breath. This could have been so much worse.

"I'm sorry," she says. "I've never had a gun pointed at me before. I was up all night dealing with police and reporters and I don't know how many lawyers called for reasons that are completely beyond me."

"How did Wally know?"

"While Chloe was supposedly getting packed, she was actually turning the light in the front bedroom on and off, signaling SOS in Morse code. Jerry saw it from his garage and went out and told Wally Roach, who was parked out on the street."

"Clever. How does she know Morse code?"

"SOS is something everybody knows."

"I don't. Wally was surprisingly good at sneaking, though I don't know why he didn't simply make his presence known and arrest the idiot."

< 200 >

"Probably he didn't want anybody to get shot."

"And look how that turned out."

"In any case, it's always best to avoid confrontation with a crazy person."

"What's going to happen to Henry?"

"Prison, I suppose. Or maybe the loony bin. What a moron. Who acts like that?" She turns into the driveway. The cool darkness of the garage is comforting.

I want to go to my room, turn off the light, and collapse in my bed. I would find some relief in a long cry. But my priority is getting thirteen hundred dollars to the mall parking lot by one o'clock. And how am I going to do that? Mom's going to be hovering all afternoon. Also, I'm woozy from lack of sleep and painkillers; only a fool would drive right now. My right arm is immobilized and the tiniest flex of my shoulder sends stabbing pain through my whole body. I've been told it'll be at least a week before I can grasp a steering wheel.

Vernon will be furious if I don't show up. He'll come here. How am I going to get this done?

Mom walks me up the stairs, follows me into my room, and helps me into bed. She actually tucks the blanket under my chin like she did when I was a little girl.

"You all set?" she asks. "Because I'm about to fall over. I've got to get some sleep or my head's going to explode."

"Thanks, Mom." My voice is groggy as I close my eyes. When I hear the door close my eyes pop right back open.

I tiptoe down the hallway, tap on Chloe's door, and enter. The room is dusky and warm. Two different snores fill the room.

"Hey." I flip on the light. "Wake up."

"What? Go away." Chloe brings her arm up to protect her eyes.

< 201 >

"I need you to run me on a quick errand. Right now. While Mom's asleep."

"No. I'm sleeping. Do you know how precious my sleep time is?"

"Your insane father shot me."

"You'll live."

"It's important. An hour, that's all I need."

She flails her way out from under the covers. Without a word she pulls her shorts on and awakens and changes Allison. The only exchange between us is when we're in the car and I tell her where to take me.

She leaves the car running while I go into the bank. Filling out the withdrawal slip is difficult because my hand is shaky from pain and exhaustion. I'm given a record of my account action. I've deposited five thousand three hundred and eighty. Not bad for a part-time minimum-wage-earning addict. I've withdrawn seven hundred and forty. And now another withdrawal of thirteen hundred, leaving me with thirty-three forty. As in addiction recovery, hoarding money is an erratic process requiring hard work, vigilance, and obsession. Progress is never easy and obstacles are never small. But I'm getting there. In this I am determined: Someday I'll move away from Caprock, a whole person, with start-over money in the bank.

Chloe remains grimly silent as she drives me to the mall. Vernon's parked in the same place he was last night. I direct Chloe to park several cars away from him. I don't want him saying things about my sister and I definitely don't want him seeing the tiny baby that's sleeping in the back.

I get out of the car and hobble toward him. Every uneven step on the hard surface sends pain shooting through my shoulder. Vernon emerges from the driver's side and takes

< 202 >

up the same leaning posture as last night. When I get close I hold out the envelope of cash.

"What the hell is going on with you?" He eyes the bandage and sling as he accepts the envelope. "You don't seem to be doing all that well up here in the panhandle. You're falling apart bit by bit."

"Tell me about it."

"When you coming back to Dallas?"

"I don't know that I ever will." I study him. What a creep. This'll probably be the last time I ever see him. When I walk away he'll be part of a past I'll never revisit.

"You need to be careful with yourself," he tells me. "I knew this guy once, well, people getting over addiction tend to go crazy on themselves, know what I mean?"

"Not even remotely."

"It's psychological. About how, because you're mad at yourself, you take risks you shouldn't take."

"Good-bye, Vernon," I say, turning back toward the car.

"Look me up next time you're in Dallas," he calls after me. "I can get you hooked up."

I'd give a farewell wave but I'm too tired to lift my arm.

"That it?" Chloe asks when I collapse into the passenger seat.

"That's it," I tell her. She drives us home. I sleep until seven o'clock.

When I go downstairs Mom and Zachary and Chloe are out on the back porch. Glasses of red wine stand on the table in front of Mom and Zachary. Chloe is sipping from a bottle of vitamin water while she nurses Allison. Also on the table is a pizza box, which is surprising because Mom disapproves of pizza. I step outside.

"Pizza? Are we having a party?" Taking the seat between

< 203 >

Mom and Chloe, I look out over the backyard. About this, at least, Zachary is right – the evenings in Caprock are comfortable.

"Just this once for a special occasion," Mom says. "We're celebrating being alive."

"You want to know something interesting?" Chloe points her half-slice of pizza at us. "I eat this pizza tonight and tomorrow Allison's poop will smell like pepperoni."

"That is interesting," I say. "Tell us more."

And even though I'm being facetious, she talks for five minutes about how what she eats determines not only the smell, but also the color and consistency, of what Allison deposits in her diaper.

It seems like it's been ages since I've had a chance to settle down for my solitary spiritual time. After all that's happened, I should probably give a few minutes to the meaning of life. So when I go up to my room I open my Bible to a center point – Obadiah 13:

Do not enter the gate of my people in the day of their disaster. Yes, you, do not gloat over their calamity in the day of their disaster. And do not loot their wealth in the day of their disaster.

Hmm. Looks like God doesn't want others messing with his people when they're down. I'm too frazzled to go any deeper. I close the Bible and go to bed.

By morning I've been offered three hundred and fifty dollars for the cars. And a bidding war for the lamp played out overnight. Starting out at six-fifty, during a period from midnight to four a.m., the price bounced between three buyers until it peaked at nine hundred. A gratifying and auspicious turn of events.

Zachary's told me not to come to work for a couple of days and the thought of hanging around the house

< 204 >

waiting for my shoulder to heal makes me crazy. I spend the morning on the couch watching lousy television and feeling sorry for myself. Mom took yesterday off but today she returned to her regular routine. Occasionally Chloe rushes through the living room, phone to her ear. She's busy requesting and filing and making phone calls about transferring for her senior year. Around eleven o'clock she and Allison join me on the couch. Glad to have company, I turn off the TV.

"What have you decided to do with the check from Allison's dad?" I ask.

"I haven't decided yet. So far this transfer is costing five hundred dollars in fees and I'm losing eight hours' credit."

"Not surprising."

"Even if I take his money it won't be long before I'm broke again."

"Chloe, you're a college student. Being broke goes with the territory."

"But now I've got Allison to take care of. I can't be broke." Despondent and burdened, she's in need of a distraction.

"There's an abandoned church in Camille," I tell her. "I'd sure like to go have a look at it." It's a hint. She knows I can't drive.

"What? No. No more invading old buildings."

"Invading implies aggression. I'm not aggressive; I'm curious. Also, it's fun."

"Olivia, I swear, you've gone from one addiction to another."

"Please?"

< 205 >

Camille

Pitted two-lane Route 66 marks Camille's southern border, with I-40 a half-mile to the south. With a population of two hundred and twenty, Camille is smaller, even, than Aimes. It doesn't even have a school or a Dairy Queen.

The town is no more than a cluster of flat brick houses surrounded by ranch land. Some of the homes have fenced-in lawns in front, with the occasional pinwheel spinning in the wind. The grass is colorless and crunchy and the pinwheels are frayed.

The acreage behind every house holds barns that need paint and broken-down farm machinery.

"Not a charming place," Chloe says.

The church's spire, topped by a solid cross, rises from the west side of the town.

Chloe does a drive-through of the streets. There are no people to be seen, but there are sulky horses behind wire fences; their ears perk and their noses turn as we pass by. Every house has at least two non-operational vehicles in the driveway – ancient cars or trucks coated with dust so thick that their color is lost. When things stop working out here they just remain where they died.

"Where is everybody?" she asks. "It's like there's been a great catastrophe and we're the only people left alive in the universe."

< 206 >

"Who lives in these houses? What draws them here? I just don't get it."

"Maybe they're ranch hands. The property is probably cheap."

"The nearest grocery store is an hour away."

"I guess there are city people and country people."

The orange brick church is smaller than it looked in the picture on the website. The high windows are all intact, but they're not stained glass. The parking area in front of the church consists of deep rough tracks carved in the mud by tires after a rain storm. Chloe bounces over them for a few feet, then comes to a stop. We both get out of the car. Strapping on the halter as she circles to the passenger side, Chloe extricates Allison from the car seat, and slides the tiny squirming body into the pouch.

The hum of traffic on the highway is distant but constant. The whistling wind pushes everything in its path toward the east. I can see how a certain kind of peace could be found here. Removed as it is from the rest of the world, there's an absence of pressure, a perception that time moves slower.

The cement steps leading to the portico are cracked. The bricks are crumbling. The windows are brown with dirt. The wooden door frame is jagged with splinters. And the double doors are padlocked.

"So what are we talking here?" Chloe shades her eyes as she squints up at the cross. "Baptist? Methodist? Presbyterian?"

"I'm not sure. Does it matter?"

I hobble around the side of the building. Chloe tromps along behind me. There's another door at the rear, also locked. Not to be deterred, I pull out my trusty screwdriver and begin to remove the knob. With my arm in a sling, it's

< 207 >

not as easy a task as it ordinarily would be, but it offers no challenge, either.

"I bet there's a special place in hell for people who break into churches," Chloe says, but she doesn't sound too worried about it.

It takes me less than five minutes to jimmy the mechanism. We step into a small dark chamber. I take quick inventory – desk and chair, two file cabinets, a bookshelf jammed with books, a shadowy closet holding a couple of dark robes. Dusty corners and moldy tomes make my nose itch.

Five steps take me to the doorway that leads to the choir loft. I look out at the sanctuary, a massive vacant cavern. Rays streak through the high dirty panes, creating rectangles of brown light. Every pew has been removed. The floor tiles are broken where the mounts were drilled out. Jagged holes gape in the ceiling where the lights once were. The only fixture left in the entire hall is the communion rail, which is so coated with dust that its stain is indiscernible.

"Wow." Chloe pushes past me, rushing to the center of the chancel and taking measure of the vast room. "Wow," she says again. Unhooking the halter, she scurries back and pushes Allison at me with the instruction, "Take this."

I don't know what most people do when confronted by a massive empty space, but apparently my little sister sings. She returns to the center point, takes a deep breath, and belts out:

"Matchmaker, matchmaker, make me a match. Find me a find. Catch me a catch!"

The sisters' song from *Fiddler on the Roof.* She was in every musical in high school. I'd forgotten; and though I was distantly aware of the fact, it never fully registered that she actually stood on a stage and sang. I was never there.

< 208 >

Not for a single performance. With Allison cradled in the crook of my good arm, I shuffle to the middle of the sanctuary so we can get the full effect.

"For Papa, make him a scholar. For Momma, make him rich as a king. For me, well, I wouldn't holler if he were as handsome as anything!"

My sister's full soprano flies without barriers, bounces off bare walls, reverberating and reverberating until her voice is as huge as a hundred voices.

"Find me no find. Catch me no catch. Unless he's a matchless match!"

She draws the last note out, stomping her foot playfully to signal the end.

"The acoustics of a huge empty hall, a vocalist's ultimate dream," she says as the echo of the last note dies away.

"I never knew you could sing like that."

"High school. Good times." She skips down the two steps to join me, adding, "And because I know lots of songs, I will always be able to come up with something to sing." She lifts Allison from my arms and twirls around.

"You girls lost?" A woman emerges from the office. With a startled squeal Chloe stops dancing. "Or did you just break into our church to have yourselves a little sing-a-long?"

About Mom's age, our visitor is shapeless and beige. Her cheeks are chapped and sunken. And her voice is low-pitched and rough. I'm going to have to stop smoking. If I don't, this is me in twenty years. I'll dry out just like this woman. My skin will look like baked lizard and my voice will sound like a man's.

"We just came to have a look," I tell her.

"Have a look at what?" She gazes around the empty sanctuary, clearly puzzled about what we might see that would be of interest.

< 209 >

"We aren't going to take anything."

"There's nothing to take. What happened to you?" She eyes me with suspicion. "Car wreck or something?"

"Something like that."

"I expect you to put that knob back on the door and lock up before you leave." She turns to go.

"Wait," I say. "Can I ask you something?"

With an annoyed sigh, she turns back and nods.

"What do you do out here? Why do you live here?"

At first her faded blue eyes squint with hostility. She doesn't like to ruminate and she doesn't like to explain. Also, maybe my question sounded critical; I didn't mean it to be. But then she tilts her head as an answer occurs to her.

"I'm here because there's plenty of space to do my thing."

"And what's your thing?"

"Come on, I'll educate you."

She turns and heads toward the back. Chloe and I follow.

"I'm Mary," she says over her shoulder. "Mary Horner, and I've lived here for over thirty years." She leads us outside and across a dirt-and-weed field to her little dried-out house.

And her thing – the pastime she's built her life around – is pygmy goats. Another type of hobby; another type of collection.

"See, some people like their meat," she tells us, "but I love the little guys, so I don't work that end of it. What I do is, I sell their milk. Not a lot of money in it, but we get along."

The goats are about half the size of other goats – that's just my guess; I'm no goat expert. They're kind of cute, with their compact bodies, weird eyes, and sweet faces, but that doesn't keep them from smelling like goats. Their pen connects to her house, which means she's right in the middle of

< 210 >

them when she steps from her back door into her backyard; and when she steps back into her house, she's tracking their crap inside. There are about twenty of them. In the back corner there's a lean-to for shade and to cover their food and water. And placed out in the pen are objects to climb on – a couple of tree stumps and several large rocks. She's created a real pygmy goat paradise.

She motions us into the pen as she opens the gate and steps inside. Chloe chooses to stay outside the fence, but I go in with Mary, who squats down and opens her arms. The goats crowd around, rubbing their faces against her shoulders and breasts. I notice she's kneeling in goat poop. Curious, several of them bump and rub against my legs. I tell them they're cute. Flies buzz all around them and when I pet their heads dust forms an odorous cloud that drifts upward, stinging my eyes and coating my face. I think I saw some sani-wipes in the glove compartment of Chloe's car.

Mary tells us everything there is to know about pygmy goats: diet, greens and grains; gestation period, five months; life expectancy, ten to fifteen years. She can claim she's happy living in the middle of nowhere, but only lonely people talk non-stop to strangers for a full hour. She doesn't ask us in, which is disappointing because I would've liked to've seen her living space. Are her kitchen counters cluttered or cleared? Which does she prefer – duvet or bedspread? Does she own a computer? A recliner? An electric toothbrush?

After we say good-bye and put the knob back on the church door, we return to the highway and head back to town.

"I just got rid of skunk," I complain, "and now I smell like goat." The four wipes I've used on my hands and face have barely made a difference in how filthy I feel.

< 211 >

"There's something I'm wondering," she says. "What are the twelve steps?"

"Six. There are six steps. One, accept that you're out of control; two, lean on a higher power; three, confide in a sponsor; four, make amends; five, replace the old life with a new one; and six, help others though their addiction recovery."

"Are you doing all that stuff?" she asks. "Is it working?"

An honest answer would disappoint her. The stripped-down truth is, I'm a broken-down truck in a country drive-way. I doubt my sincerity as regards the recovery steps. I try to communicate with a higher power, but it seems hypo-critical when I'm not even sure I believe in one. I'm in debt and I'm stashing secret money. I'm keeping secrets from my mother and my therapist. I'm disingenuous with my parole officer. I'm sneaking and stealing.

Am I making progress? Yes, in my recovery, I am; and it's slow and it's difficult. But my goal is to get better, not to be better. Maybe in the future I'll be wise, generous, and pro-ductive; but at this point, I am what I am – a self-absorbed addict with murky morals. Chloe was right when she said I've traded one addiction for another. Slipping into build-ings, taking things and selling them, watching my bank account grow – these aren't things a good person does. But they're things I do.

"That goat milk she was talking about," I say, changing the subject. "It's not pasteurized. I didn't see any sanitary facility. She milks those goats right there in that pen sur-rounded by feces and goat hair."

"Well, that can't be legal. Somebody should call the public health people."

"You do it. You like to report things."

The next morning, even though I'm not supposed to

< 212 >

drive, and even though driving hurts, I go back out to the Meskar place with two backpacks. Crawling under the fence and hiking to the house makes me sweaty and shaky. I'm physically unable to pull myself on to the deck from the ladder, so I go against the urbexers' code by waggling the lock of one of the downstairs windows and scrambling in over the sill. And I go through the house and pick up everything of value that isn't prohibitively heavy or bulky – an ornate silver chafing dish, a very old diamond Rolex, a string of pearls, a miniature carriage clock, a 1937 edition of the Steinbeck novel, *Of Mice and Men*, a cloisonné egg, and a pair of Grey Walker engravings. Because of my injured right side, I sling both heavy backpacks over my left shoulder. Hunching and lurching back to the car with the lopsided burden, I cast a grotesque shadow.

When I get back to town I stop by Penny Rittenhauer's house and drop Eubert Meskar's will in her mailbox.

< 213 >

Acknowledgements

Olivia's struggle against addiction is loosely based on a friend's experience. He faced his ordeal with equanimity and humor, though I'm sure at times he must have been miserable, disappointed, and humbled. Thanks, Jay, for the inspiration.

I'd like to acknowledge the Singapore American Women's Association's Writers' Group, a supportive circle of friends who listened and advised, and put up with the way I read so fast with my Texas accent. Special thanks to Teresa Zink, who introduced me to my agent: in a business that's often competitive and stingy with contacts, Teresa is generous when it comes to making introductions and helping other writers meet their goals.

I recognize and recommend the MFA program of Fairleigh-Dickinson, which nurtured my ability, process, confidence, and dedication – especially Ellen Akins, who is a gifted writer, reviewer, and editor. She is my encourager and I'm honored to call her my friend.

Also, thanks to my agent, Helen Mangham, of the Jacaranda Literary Agency, who is dedicated to writers and literature; and the people at Arcadia – Joe Harper, Piers Russell-Cobb, and my editor, Helen Francis, who is insightful and sharp.

< 215 >